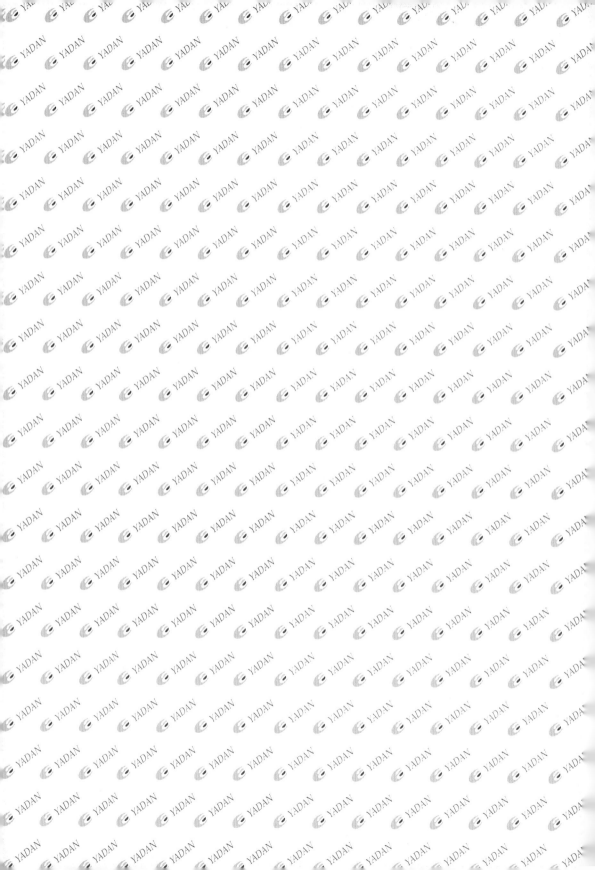

張文娟 著

中級
Listening
Comprehension
& Speaking

NEW

新制全民英檢

GEPT

The General English Proficiency Test [Intermediate]

聽力&口說 模擬試題
+解答

CONTENTS
目錄

第一章
前言

第二章
聽力講座

第三章
口說能力講座

第四章
聽力模擬試題

CONTENTS
目錄

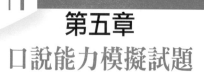

第五章
口說能力模擬試題

第六章
520 個最常考的中級字彙

CHAPTER

1

前言

中級 Listening Comprehension & Speaking

NEW

新制全民英檢

GEPT

The General English Proficiency Test [Intermediate]

聽力&口說 模擬試題 +解答

1. 關於全民英檢 [中級]：
聽力 & 口説的問與答（Q&A）

Q：「全民英語能力分級檢定測驗」的由來？

A：在國際化的趨勢下，推展全民英語學習運動已成為教育界及民間普遍的共識，而語言訓練測驗中心多年來辦理外語能力測驗的經驗也顯示國內需要一套完整並具公信力之英語能力分級檢定系統，以適應各級教育及社會各階層的需求，因此在 86 年度邀集國內相關領域之學者專家成立研究及諮詢委員會，開始著手研發這項測驗系統，希望能夠提供國內各階段英語學習者公平、可靠、具效度的英語能力評量工具。教育部為落實「終身學習」的教育理念，及推動全民學外語的政策，於 88 年 3 月起 3 年間撥款補助「全民英檢」的研發。

Q：這項測驗各級數命題方向為何？考生應如何準備？

A：「全民英檢」各級數的命題方向均參考國內各級英語教育之課程大綱，同時也廣泛蒐集相關教材進行內容分析，以求命題內容能符合國內各級英語教育指標。此外，這項測驗的內容反映本土的生活經驗與特色，因此命題內容生活化，並包含流行話題及時事。這項測驗並未針對特定領域或教材命題，但因各級數測驗均包含聽、說、讀、寫四部分，而目前國內英語教育仍偏重讀與寫，因此平日考生必須加強聽、說訓練，同時多接觸英語媒體（如報章雜誌、廣播、電視、電影、網站等），以求在測驗時能有較好的表現。

Q：通過「全民英檢」合格標準者是否取得合格證書？又合格證書有何用途或效力？

A：是的，語言訓練測驗中心將於寄發複試成績單時一併寄發合格證書給通過「全民英檢」之聽、說、讀、寫四項測驗者。目前「全民英檢」已經為全國公務人員陞任加分、教育部公費留考、中研院國際研究生學程及大學甄選入學招生採用，並獲中華航空公司、台北捷運公司、台灣金融研訓院、長榮航空、國泰金融集團等多家公民營及金融機構採認作為人力評估及招募人才之參考，此外，中山、中央、中正、中興、台大、台師大、交大、成大、政大與清大等多所大學及高中亦採用作為學習成果評量或畢業檢核依據。

Q：「全民英檢」中級之檢測程度為何？

A：中級具有使用簡單英語進行日常生活溝通的能力，相當於高中畢業程度。

中級 Listening Comprehension & Speaking
新制全民英檢 NEW
GEPT 聽力&口說 模擬試題 +解答
The General English Proficiency Test [Intermediate]

Q：「全民英檢」中級之分數如何計算？

A：聽力及閱讀能力測驗成績計分方式採標準計分。如以傳統粗分計分概念來說，以「中級」為例，聽力測驗每題 2.67 分，閱讀測驗每題 3 分，各項得分為答對題數乘以每題分數，可以大概計算是否通過「中級」初試。考生成績將根據粗分，透過統計方式微調，使歷次測驗的成績可以直接進行比較。寫作及口說能力測驗成績採整體式評分（初級、中級、中高級），使用級分制，分為 0~5 級分，再轉換成百分制。複試各項成績均達 80 分（初級寫作為 70 分）以上，視為通過。

Q：寫作及口說測驗既採非選擇題方式，評分方式為何？

A：寫作及口說能力測驗採人工閱卷，每位考生的作答均經由受過訓練的合格評分老師評閱，評分係根據「全民英檢」各級數寫作／口說能力測驗分數說明，經初、複審程序進行。評分期間並有專人持續追蹤評分老師的評分情形，確認每位評分老師均穩定掌握評分指標。

Q：初試（聽力、閱讀）成績要達幾分才較可能通過複試（寫作、口說）？

A：英語學習者在聽、說、讀、寫四項語言技能上的表現上會互有差異，而寫作與口說又是一般國人感到較困難的項目。根據本中心的統計，過去幾年多數通過複試並取得「全民英檢」合格證書的考生，其聽力與閱讀測驗的平均成績均高達 100 分（各項滿分為 120 分）；

而平均未達 90 分者，複試的通過率僅約一成。因此，通過初試但平均低於 90 分者，除非在參加複試前，英語能力有明顯的提昇，否則通過複試的機率較不高。

Q：考後會公布試題及答案嗎？

A：增進英語能力需要持之以恆，長時間練習，為避免誤導考生以為反覆練習試題是英語能力進步的捷徑，舉凡國際間大型、知名的測驗如 TOEFL、IELTS 等，皆未公布每次測驗試題，「全民英檢」亦經諮詢委員會決議，不逐一公布歷次測驗試題。惟為提供報考者於試前熟悉題型及練習的機會，語言訓練測驗中心會擇適當時機公佈部分試題，至 98 年已公布初、中、中高級各 4 套試題。

Q：可不可以知道自己錯在哪裡？

A：本測驗為標準參照測驗，功能係評量考生英語能力是否已達各級數參考效標，並非診斷測驗，無法提供作答錯誤資料分析及錯誤更正說明。

Q：合格證書有期限嗎？

A：證書永久有效，惟欲申請加發合格證書或成績單須於測驗日起 2 年內提出（非指證書的效期為 2 年），逾期申請無法受理。有關成績採用與否及採認年限等規定請直接洽詢成績採用單位。

中級 Listening Comprehension & Speaking NEW
新制全民英檢
GEPT 聽力&口說 模擬試題 +解答
The General English Proficiency Test [Intermediate]

Q：合格證書須自行申請嗎？如欲補發／加發該如何申請？

A：合格證書將隨成績單寄給通過複試者，毋須提出申請。欲自費申請補發／加發成績單、初試通過證明或合格證書，需自測驗日起2年內為之，超過2年者恕無法受理。

Q：工作單位或學校只要求通過聽力、閱讀兩項測驗，除成績單外，有其他證明文件嗎？

A：語言訓練測驗中心考後主動寄發之初試成績單，除明列聽力及閱讀能力測驗成績外，兩項成績達通過標準者另註明「達初試通過標準」。為因應部分考生要求，自98年起受理考生自行依所需付費申請「初試通過證明」。

2. 各級能力說明

➥綜合能力說明：

初級（Elementary）

具有基礎英語能力，能理解和使用淺易日常用語。

建議下列人員宜具有該級英語能力：

一般行政助理、維修技術人員、百貨業、餐飲業、旅館業或觀光景點服務人員、計程車駕駛等。

中級（Intermediate）

具有使用簡單英語進行日常生活溝通的能力。

建議下列人員宜具有該級英語能力：

一般行政、業務、技術、銷售人員、護理人員、旅館／飯店接待人員、總機人員、警政人員、旅遊從業人員等。

中級 Listening Comprehension & Speaking

NEW

新制全民英檢

GEPT

The General English Proficiency Test [Intermediate]

聽力&口說 模擬試題 +解答

中高級（High-Intermediate）

英語能力逐漸成熟，應用的領域擴大，雖有錯誤，但無礙溝通。

建議下列人員宜具有該級英語能力：

商務、企劃人員、祕書、工程師、研究助理、空服人員、航空機師、航管人員、海關人員、導遊、外事警政人員、新聞從業人員、資訊管理人員等。

高級（Advanced）

英語流利順暢，僅有少許錯誤，應用能力擴及學術或專業領域。

建議下列人員宜具有該級英語能力：

高級商務人員、協商談判人員、英語教學人員、研究人員、翻譯人員、外交人員、國際新聞從業人員等。

優級（Superior）

英語能力接近受過高等教育之母語人士，各種場合均能使用適當策略作最有效的溝通。

建議下列人員宜具有該級英語能力：

專業翻譯人員、國際新聞特派人員、外交官員、協商談判主談人員等。

➥各級分項能力說明：

初級

聽：能聽懂與日常生活相關的淺易談話，包括價格、時間及地點等。

讀：可看懂與日常生活相關的淺易英文，並能閱讀路標、交通標誌、招牌、簡單菜單、時刻表及賀卡等。

說：能朗讀簡易文章、簡單地自我介紹，對熟悉的話題能以簡易英語對答，如問候、購物、問路等。

寫：能寫簡單的句子及段落，如寫明信片、便條、賀卡及填表格等。對一般日常生活相關的事物，能以簡短的文字敘述或說明。

中級

聽：在日常生活中，能聽懂一般的會話；能大致聽懂公共場所廣播、氣象報告及廣告等。在工作時，能聽懂簡易的產品介紹與操作說明。能大致聽懂外籍人士的談話及詢問。

讀：在日常生活中，能閱讀短文、故事、私人信件、廣告、傳單、簡介及使用說明等。在工作時，能閱讀工作須知、公告、操作手冊、例行的文件、傳真、電報等。

說：在日常生活中，能以簡易英語交談或描述一般事物，能介紹

自己的生活作息、工作、家庭、經歷等，並可對一般話題陳 述看法。在工作時，能進行簡單的答詢，並與外籍人士交談 溝通。

　　寫：能寫簡單的書信、故事及心得等。對於熟悉且與個人經歷相關的主題，能以簡易的文字表達。

中高級

　　聽：在日常生活中，能聽懂社交談話，並能大致聽懂一般的演講、
　　報導及節目等。在工作時，能聽懂簡報、討論、產品介紹及 操作說明等。

　　讀：在日常生活中，能閱讀書信、說明書及報章雜誌等。在工作
　　時，能閱讀一般文件、摘要、會議紀錄及報告等。

　　說：在日常生活中，對與個人興趣相關的話題，能流暢地表達意見及看法。在工作時，能接待外籍人士、介紹工作內容、洽 談業務、在會議中發言，並能做簡報。

　　寫：能寫一般的工作報告及書信等。除日常生活相關主題外，與工作相關的事物、時事及較複雜或抽象的概念皆能適當表達。

高級

　　聽：在日常生活中，能聽懂各類主題的談話、辯論、演講、報導及節目等。在工作時，參與業務會議或談判時，能聽懂報告及討論的內容。

讀：能閱讀各類不同主題、體裁的文章，包括報章雜誌、文學作品、專業期刊、學術著作及文獻等。

說：對於各類主題皆能流暢地表達看法、參與討論，能在一般會議或專業研討會中報告或發表意見等。

寫：能寫一般及專業性摘要、報告、論文、新聞報導等，可翻譯一般書籍及新聞等。對各類主題均能表達看法，並作深入探討。

優級

聽：能聽懂各類主題及體裁的內容，理解程度與受過高等教育之母語人士相當。

讀：能閱讀各類不同主題、體裁文章。閱讀速度及理解程度與受過高等教育之母語人士相當。

說：能在各種不同場合以正確流利之英語表達看法；能適切引用文化知識及慣用語詞。

寫：能撰寫不同性質的文章，如企劃報告、專業/學術性摘要、論文、新聞報導及時事評論等。對於各類主題均能有效完整地闡述並作深入探討。

以上摘錄自全民英檢官網

中級 Listening Comprehension & Speaking

NEW

新制全民英檢
GEPT

The General English Proficiency Test [Intermediate]

聽力&口說 模擬試題 +解答

CHAPTER 2

聽力講座

中級 Listening Comprehension & Speaking

NEW

新制全民英檢

GEPT
The General English Proficiency Test [Intermediate]

聽力&口說 模擬試題 +解答

1. 平日培養英語聽力的方法

　　相較於讀和寫，在台灣學英語，沒有自然聽到英語的環境，不過這是在非英語系國家學英語都會遇到的問題，還是要靠自己花心思多創造聽得到英語的機會，儘量自我訓練聽力。因為中文和英文差異非常大，所以對台灣學生來說，要聽懂英語更加有難度，必須要花不少的時間和精力來掌握英語的聽力。

　　英語是拼音的語言，既然如此，從聽力來著手學習這個外語，才是省時省力的上策，以下是一些可以供參考的聽力訓練方法：

☆多聽模擬試題

☆多聽廣播教學節目的對話

☆多聽廣播和電視的英語新聞報導

☆多看英語節目和英語影集與電影，同時多注意聽口語用法

☆善用網路資源，例如 YouTube、TED 等

☆邊聽邊記，快速記下主題和關鍵字，仔細聆聽完畢後，試著用所記下的速記筆記來覆述內容。

2. 如何針對全民英檢中級聽力作準備

　　本測驗分三部分，全為四選一之選擇題，共 45 題，作答時間約 30 分鐘。

第一部分：看圖辨義

　　共 15 題，試題冊上有數幅圖畫，每一圖畫有 1 ～ 3 個描述該圖的題目，每題請聽光碟放音機播出題目以及四個英語敍述之後，選出與所看到的圖畫最相符的答案，每題只播出一遍。

☆本部分常考的問題如下：

(1) 動作：例如描述圖中人物在進行的活動。

(2) 細節：例如描述衣著、外表、地點、位置、天氣、食物、交通工具等。

(3) 職業：由圖中人物的工作來判斷其職業。

(4) 比較：通常為價格或數目的比較級和最高級。

(5) 推論：例如營業時間和行程表等。

☆技巧：

(1) 在還沒有播出問題和四個選項前，一定要先快速看此題的圖畫，同時預測題目的主題和內容，還有可能會聽到的問題和選項。看圖片時，要特別注意圖中的人名、數字、標示箭頭等，才不會遺漏作答相關的指示。

(2) 因為每題播出內容的速度為正常速度，對考生而言可能非常

快，作答的速度要儘量跟上，作答完一題，要馬上接下來看下
一題的圖畫，不要因為這一題答案無法決定，停頓下來，而錯
過下一題的播音。

★準備方法：

(1) 熟悉日常生活的詞彙：本部分所考的多為日常生活情境會出
現的詞彙，因此在參加聽力測驗前，務必要熟悉日常生活中的常
用字彙與慣用語，掌握常用詞彙的正確發音，平日很少聽英語
或開口唸生字的考生，可能會因為無法正確辨音而聽不出某些
詞彙，因而在聽力測驗平白失分。

(2) 培養辨音能力：英語中有許多字讀音相近，意思卻完全不同，
若不能正確分辨，極易造成聽力理解上的困難，尤其是某
些同音異義字（Homophone），例如：eye, I; coarse, course;
for, four; pair, pear 等，發音相同，但是意義完全不同。
因此在聆聽英語內容時，一定要專心分辨字音與字義。

(3) 熟悉連音的現象：母語人士在以常速說話時，經常出現連音
的現象，因此常造成非母語人士聽力理解上的障礙。連音發生的
必要條件如下：

1. 必須在同一個意群 (thought group) 中的單字之間，方可產生連
音。

2. 當前一個字的字尾是子音，後一個字的字首是母音，此二音

中級 Listening Comprehension & Speaking
新制全民英檢 NEW
GEPT 聽力&口說 模擬試題+解答
The General English Proficiency Test [Intermediate]

連唸形成連音。

　　以下是兩個連音現象的例子：

◎ A：What are you going to do this weekend?

　　B：I'm going to visit my aunt. How <u>about you</u>?

　　　　　　　　　　　　　　　　　　　[chu]

◎ <u>Care about us.</u>

　　[kɛr əbaʊt əs] 變為 [kɛrəbaʊtəs]

(4) 掌握句子的重音部分：英文中有兩類字，第一類為「內容字」 (content word)，是有內容的字，帶了資訊，這類的詞包括名詞、動詞、形容詞、副詞；而另一類的詞為「功能字」 (function word)，只是文法結構上需要的字，通常這些字不帶什麼重要的資訊，如冠詞 (article)、代名詞 (pronoun)、介系詞 (preposition) 等，都屬於只有文法功能的字。通常一個句子的重音落在「內容字」上，而「功能字」只要輕唸即可，同樣要加重的有疑問詞 (who,what,where,when,why,how) 和否定詞 (not,neither)，因為他們都代表一個句子中的重要資訊。例如：

1. The rain in Spain stays mainly in the plain.

2. He is NOT coming to this party on Saturday.

在第一句中有劃線的字屬於「內容字」，因此要發重音，其它的字只要輕唸就好。如果聽清楚了一個句子中的「內容字」，通常便能了解這句話的主旨。

(5) 語調：同一個句子經常可能因為語調的不同，表達的意思也有所不同，因此在聆聽的時候，必須要注意語調。例如：

(A) He lost his job again.

(B) He lost his job again?

在 (A) 這個句子中，句子結尾處語調向下，是陳述句，表達一個事實；但是在 (B) 句中，結尾處語調向上，則是問句，表達一個問題，也有非常詫異，想要求證的意思。

第二部分：問答

　　共 15 題，每題請聽光碟放音機播出一英語問句或直述句之後，從試題冊上 A、B、C、D 四個回答或回應中，選出一個最適合者作答。每題只播出一遍。

☆本部分常考的問題如下：

　　(1) 問句：包括以 who、what、when、where、why 和 how 為首（含 how much、how often、how long 等）的問句，還有 Yes-No 問句。

　　(2) 直述句：通常為説話者陳述自己觀點，希望獲得對方的看法。

☆技巧：

　　(1) 在還沒有播出問題前，先快速瀏覽四個選項，猜測可能會出現的主題。

　　(2) 在聆聽時如果遇到聽不懂的生字或片語，不要著慌，依情境猜測整個問句的最可能含意，選出最合理的答案後，繼續下一 題，千萬不要被某一題絆住，因而耽誤到了下一題的作答。

☆準備方法：

(1) 熟悉日常對話的用語：此項目是要測驗對話能力，所以要選出的答案必須是最合情合理的答話。

(2) 培養預測能力：聆聽問話前先快速瀏覽四個選項，在問題還未播出前，推測題目的主題和內容。

(3) 迅速掌握關鍵字：在看選項和聽問話時，要能快速聽出關鍵訊息所在。

(4) 聽懂言外之意：有時聽懂了問句的每個字，但是卻不知整句話要表達什麼，這時就只能憑語感來推論可能的言外之意，然後挑選出最可能的反應。

(5) 正確推論生字：聽到生字還是能不慌不忙，依照問句可能的語意來推測生字含義，然後繼續下一題的作答。

(6) 熟悉語調：完全熟悉口語中語調不同所表達的不同意義，聽懂連音和重音的現象。

中級 Listening Comprehension & Speaking
新制全民英檢 NEW
GEPT 聽力&口說 模擬試題+解答
The General English Proficiency Test [Intermediate]

第三部分：簡短對話

　　共 15 題，每題請聽光碟放音機播出一段對話及一個相關的問題後，從試題冊上 A、B、C、D 四個選項中選出一個最適合者作答。每段對話及問題只播出一遍。

　　☆本部分常考的問題如下：

　　(1) 主旨題：通常要測驗學生對整段對話大意的了解，也就是談話的主題。例如：

　　"What are the man and the woman talking about?"

　　「這位男士和這位女士在談什麼？」

　　(2) 場景題：問這段對話最可能在什麼地方出現或說話者的身分和職業等。例如：

　　"Where did this conversation most likely take place?"

　　「這段對話最可能在什麼地方出現？」

　　(3) 細節題：測驗對話中重要的細節，例如：

　　"Will the plane tomorrow be canceled?"

　　「明天的班機是否會取消？」

　　(4) 推論題：所要測驗的項目，必須要依照所聽到的資訊推論才能得到答案，有時還會有弦外之音。例如：

　　"What did the teacher think of the result of that student's English test?"

「老師覺得那個學生的英文考試結果怎麼樣？」

☆技巧：

(1) 在還沒有播出對話前，先快速瀏覽四個選項，推測可能會出現的主題和相關問題。

(2) 如果有一題不太確定答案，不要著慌，依情境猜測一個最可能的答案後，繼續下一題的作答，千萬不要因為一直想著某一題，而耽誤了瀏覽下一題的四個選項和聆聽下一題對話的時機。

☆準備方法：

(1) 熟悉日常生活的用語：平時就要掌握實用會話的字彙和慣用語，尤其是台灣場景中的常見字彙，這些詞彙經常就是對話中的關鍵字，而且常分散出現在對話上下文中，還會以同義詞形式出現，平日要多訓練自己理解並串聯這些表達方式，才能完全理解對話內容。

(2) 培養預測能力：聆聽對話前先快速瀏覽四個選項，在問題還未播出前，推測題目的主題和內容。

(3) 訓練自己速記的技巧：只要用自己懂得的符號和系統來做速記，配合剛掃讀過的四個選項，速記下考題所要測驗的資訊即可。

(4) 聽懂言外之意：表達的方式和說話者的身分和場景密切相關，經常會有非字面上的另一層意思，多練習聆聽教學節目中母語人士的

英語對話，便能多明白這類暗喻之意。

　　(5) 不慌不忙推測生字：遇到生字能夠依對話情境和上下文推測其最可能的含義，而不會因此恐慌，以至於無法繼續聽下去。

　　(6) 熟悉語感：完全熟悉連音和重音的現象，還有口語中語調的運用。

　　希望本書的讀者能夠靈活運用以上的技巧，這樣不但可以大幅提高全民英檢的分數，也可以在實際生活中看到自己聽力程度的進步，享受擁有高級英語聽力所帶來的好處。

CHAPTER

3

口說能力講座

1. 平日培養英語口說能力的方法

　　在台灣因為聽到英語的機會受限，因此英語口說能力的發展也相對較受限，因為學習語言時，有效聲音材料的輸入和輸出是息息相關的，不過，雖然如此，還是有很多方法可以趁現在先打下穩固的基礎，等到將來有大量練習口語能力的機會時（例如出國遊學或打工度假期間），便能發揮英語實力，展現出高水準的英語會話能力。這項考試的口說能力測驗並不難，以下是一些值得推薦的準備方法：

　　☆跟讀有聲教材的內容，例如在聽英語教學 CD 時，出聲跟著老師朗讀課文，以掌握語調和重音、連音，培養語感。

　　☆錄下自己的朗讀，練習對著錄音設備獨自說英語，錄完後放出來聽，比較和英語教學 CD 內老師的朗讀有什麼不同。

　　☆隨時在腦中練習用英語對答，也可以自問自答。

　　☆和程度相近的同學組成英語會話小組，針對特定主題，練習問答的反應速度和流暢度。

　　☆把握和英語老師和母語人士練習的機會，注意被糾正的發音錯誤，例如單字的重音和發音。

　　☆善用網路資源，例如透過 skype 與國外母語人士練習英語會話，如果有聽不清楚的地方，請對方將生字或連音現象以打字方式拼出來。

2. 如何針對全民英檢中級口說能力作準備

　　本測驗分三部分，全程以錄音方式進行，共約 15 分鐘。作答說明除了印在試卷上，同時也經由耳機播出。作答說明一律為中文。採整體式評分 (0~5 級分)，評分重點包括切題度、可解度、字彙與語法、發音、語調與流利度等。

級分	分數	說明
5	100	發音清晰、正確，語調正確、自然；對應內容切題，表達流暢；語法、字彙使用自如，雖仍偶有錯誤，但無礙溝通。
4	80	發音大致清晰、正確，語調大致正確、自然；對應內容切題，語法、定彙之使用雖有錯誤，但無礙溝通。
3	60	發音、語調時有錯誤，因而影響聽者對其語意的瞭解。已能掌握基本句型結構，語法仍有錯誤；且因字彙、片語有限，阻礙表達。

| 2 | 40 | 發音、語調錯誤均多，朗讀時常因缺乏辨識能力而略過不讀；因語法、字彙常有錯誤，而無法進行有效的溝通。 |
| 1 | 20 | 發音、語調錯誤多且嚴重，又因語法錯誤甚多，認識之單字片語有限，無法清楚表達，幾乎無溝通能力。 |

☆整體技巧：

首先要熟悉面對錄音器材說英語，最佳的方法就是想像你在面對某人說英語，充滿自信地用英語表達自己的看法。因為每題的錄音時間有限，所以要善用時間，儘量於規定時間內答題完畢，如果某題的答題時間已到，便不要再繼續說下去，而影響到接下來的題答表現和情緒，評分老師不會因此而扣你的分數。

☆以下是針對各測驗項目的準備和應考技巧：

第一部分：朗讀短文

請先利用 1 分鐘的時間閱讀下面幾篇短文，閱讀時請不要發出聲音，然後在 2 分鐘內以正常的速度，清楚正確地讀出下面的短文。

☆技巧：

(1) 在這個項目中，你有一分鐘閱讀和兩分鐘朗讀短文，所以要斟酌時間，好好表現。在閱讀文章的時候，首先要判斷文意和目的，像是報章雜誌的新聞報導和讀者投書就會有非常不同的朗讀表現方式，因此我們必須要針對不同文體與其不同的讀者對象，來掌握適當的口吻和語氣，從從容容以正常速度來朗讀所給的文章。

(2) 如果遇到了不是很有把握的地方，例如不熟悉的單字或數字唸法，可以放慢速度，但是不要忽然停頓下來，或是多次重複某個字，這樣都會影響到整體的流暢度，也可能會造成聽者理解上的困難，也就很可能會被評分老師扣分了。

第二部分：回答問題

共 10 題。題目已事先錄音，每題經由耳機播出二次，不印在試卷上。第 1 至 5 題，每題回答時間 15 秒；第 6 至 10 題，每題回答時間 30 秒。每題播出後，請立即回答。回答時，不一定要用完整的句子，但請在作答時間內儘量的表達。

技巧：

(1) 本項目有回答時間 15 秒和 30 秒的兩類問題，因此要依照問題的內容和長短來作答，不要答得太短，尤其是回答 Yes-No 問句時，答案要多加補充。

(2) 所問的問題大多是日常生活中的常見問題，而且很多是和學校生活相關的問題，因此平日就要儲備好字彙量和慣用語，考場上一聽到問題，馬上就能聯想到相關的表達方式。

(3) 答案只要合情合理，並不一定要是真正的答案。

(4) 回答時不要求快，只要自自然然以正常速度回答即可。

第三部分：看圖敘述

下面有一張圖片及數個相關的問題，請先利用 30 秒的時間看圖及問題，再於 1 分半內完成作答。作答時，請直接回答，不需將題號及題目唸出。

☆本部分常考的圖片如下：

(1) 圖表告示：例如購物中心特價告示和行程表等。
(2) 動作圖：例如問圖中的交通狀況或圖中人物在做什麼。
(3) 職業圖：例如問圖中人物的職業工作。
(4) 背景圖：例如問圖中背景所在和天候如何等問題。

☆技巧：

(1)在本項目中，你有 30 秒看完圖片和問題，1.5 分鐘來完成作答，因此在看圖片的時候，馬上要在腦海中搜尋與圖片內容的相關字彙，平時可以多看圖畫字典來準備，這樣在考試時聯想起來才會快。

(2) 通常使用現在式或現在進行式，在某些情況下，也可用過去式和過去進行式表達，例如跌倒受傷等場面。

(3) 儘量用你所想得到的相關字彙來描述圖片，如果有不會的單字，則用已知的同義字或另一種方式來表達。

(4) 先描述圖片的主要內容，例如某個家庭在公園野餐，然後仔細描述你所看到的更多細節，例如天氣晴朗而且百花齊開，旁邊還有烤肉設施等。

(5) 要以正常速度來答題，力求清晰，不要以為講得越快就會顯得更流暢，能讓聽者完全明白才是最重要的。

希望本書的讀者能夠不嫌麻煩，勤練以上的口語基本功，這樣不但可以於全民英檢獲得高分，更可以在實際生活中看到自己會話能力的大幅進步，輕鬆用英語與人溝通。

中級 Listening Comprehension & Speaking NEW

新制全民英檢

GEPT

The General English Proficiency Test [Intermediate]

聽力&口說 模擬試題 +解答

CHAPTER

4

聽力模擬試題

※ 本章共包含三回聽力模擬試題

中級 Listening Comprehension & Speaking

新制全民英檢

GEPT

The General English Proficiency Test | Intermediate |

聽力&口說 模擬試題 +解答

NEW

第一回聽力模擬試題
中級聽力測驗模擬試題 -1

英語能力分級檢定測驗中級

聽力測驗

　　本測驗分三部分，全為四選一之選擇題，每部分各 15 題，共 45 題。本測驗總分 100 分，平均每題 2.2 分，作答時間約 30 分鐘。

第一部分：看圖辨義

　　本部分共 15 題，試題冊上有數幅圖畫，每一圖畫有 1 ～ 3 個描述該圖之題目，每題請聽錄音機播出題目以及 A、B、C、D 四個英語敘述之後，選出與所看到的圖畫最相符的答案，每題只播出一遍。

　　例：（看）

（聽）What is this?

A. This is a desk.

B. This is a chair.

C. This is a box.

D. This is a bed.

正確答案為 A，請在答案紙上塗黑作答。

中級 Listening Comprehension & Speaking
NEW
新制全民英檢
GEPT
The General English Proficiency Test | Intermediate |
聽力&口說 模擬試題 +解答

A.

The Schedule of Dental Services

	Mon	Tue	Wed	Thu	Fri	Sat
9:30~12:00	V		V	V	V	V
14:00~18:00	V	V	V	V	V	
19:00~21:30	V	V				

V : open

B.

$x + 3y =$
$4x + 2z =$
$2z - y =$

C.

$120 $70 $199 $120

D.

E.

F.

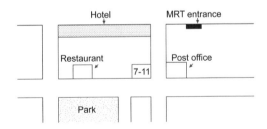

G.

H.

I.

KIDS CLOTHES   From :
DISCOUNT 10/31/2013

all prices reduced by 30%

for this sale

第二部分：問答

本部分共 15 題，每題請聽錄音機播出一英語問句或直述句之後，從試題冊上 A、B、C、D 四個回答或回應中，找出一個最適合的作答。每題只播出一遍。

例：

（聽）Where is your brother now?

（看）A. He's 20 years old.

B. He's a doctor.

C. He's thirsty.

D. He's in New York.

正確答案為 D，請在答案紙上塗黑作答。

16. A. I'm doing my homework.

B. I'm doing all right,and you?

C. I'm doing this for you.

D. I'm doing exercise.

17. A. This week has been a busy week.

B. I won't have time this weekend.

C. Don't work too much on weekends.

D. I went mountain climbing.

18. A. Let me cook dinner for you.

    B. About 3 times in a week.

    C. I enjoy dinner time with my family.

    D. Who are you cooking dinner for?

19. A. Not yet. How about you?

    B. Have you booked a room there?

    C. All hotels are full at the moment.

    D. I am not good at cooking.

20. A. I'm happy for you.

    B. Wait for me in the lobby.

    C. Singing and dancing.

    D. His hobbies are unusual.

21. A. Yes,I like the seafood there.

    B. Yes,I like the pandas there.

    C. No,I'll buy a cat.

    D. No,you can play with my dogs.

22. A. Yes,please don't let him down.

    B. No,please calm him down.

    C. Yes,please write down my telephone number.

    D. No,please write me back.

23. A. I can show you around this post office.

    B. We are busy closing the post office.

    C. You can post this notice in the office.

    D. At 18：00 every day during the week.

24. A. Did you go abroad last summer,too?

    B. I'll take intensive English lessons.

    C. I went to Japan last summer.

    D. Thank you for inviting me.

25. A. I work out in a gym.

    B. I prefer yoga to Tai Chi.

    C. I am into dancing.

    D. About 1 hour every day.

26. A. Do you work here?

    B. How can I help you?

C. Yes,over there.

D. Yes,it is not far from this convenient store.

27. A. Sorry to be late again.

　　B. Usually I ride a bike to school.

　　C. Our school bus broke down again.

　　D. Pick me up at 7：30.

28. A. My major problem is health.

　　B. I'd like to work in a college.

　　C. There are too many colleges.

　　D. English literature.

29. A. I'd like to communicate with foreigners.

　　B. Yes,I really want to learn English well.

　　C. Never,but I'd love to.

　　D. No,I don't enjoy learning English.

30. A. Have you taken a break this year?

　　B. Let me break it down for you.

　　C. Next month we'll have a short break.

　　D. What! It's been more than 2 hours!

第三部分：簡短對話

本部分共 15 題，每題請聽錄音機播出一段對話及一個相關的問題後，從試題冊上 A、B、C、D 四個備選答案中找出一個最適合的回答。每段對話及問題只播出一遍。

例：（聽）(Man)How do you go to school every day?

(Woman)Usually on foot. Sometimes by bus.

(Question)How does the woman go to school?

（看）A. She always walks to school.

B. She usually takes a bus.

C. She either walks or takes a bus.

D. She usually goes on foot,never by bus.

正確答案為 C，請在答案紙上塗黑作答。

31. A. He is a math teacher.

B. He wants students to talk only in English.

C. He gives many tests and homework.

D. He has a bad personality.

32. A. In a bank.

    B. In a restaurant.

    C. In a post office.

    D. In a travel agency.

33. A. Listening to radio news.

    B. Latest magazines.

    C. Ways of improving English.

    D. Listening to news on the Internet.

34. A. She is from a poor family.

    B. She has never been abroad.

    C. She is from a small village.

    D. She did very well in English.

35. A. His head is clearest in the morning.

    B. He has no time during the day.

    C. He learns vocabulary whenever he can.

    D. He has a test every morning.

36. A. She went there to visit a friend.

    B. She went there to get some flowers.

    C. She had an accident yesterday.

    D. She went there to have a check-up.

37. A. She is going to work with him.

    B. She has worked for a long time.

    C. She likes a bird very much.

    D. She heard the news from somebody.

38. A. She should visit Tam Shui.

    B. She should visit the Palace Museum.

    C. She should be on the top of the Taipei 101.

    D. She should sign up for a tour in Taipei.

39. A. To go to the funeral.

    B. To not attend class for a day.

    C. To look after her mother.

    D. To visit her mother in a hospital.

40. A. She agreed to take care of the cake.

    B. She'll make a deal with the bakery.

    C. She does not like the idea.

    D. She does not have money for the cake.

41. A. He went to a clinic.

    B. He had a prescription from his doctor.

    C. He worked out and ate carefully.

    D. He lost track of his weight.

NEW

Listening
Comprehension
& Speaking

中級
新制全民英檢
GEPT
The General English Proficiency Test | Intermediate |

聽力&口說 模擬試題
+解答

42. A. Overwork herself.

    B. Depend too much on him.

    C. Ask him for directions.

    D. Enjoy her break.

43. A. He is sure she can make it happen.

    B. He thinks the woman dreams too much.

    C. He seems to be a fortune teller.

    D. He dreams to be a journalist,too.

44. A. To learn how to make clothes.

    B. To donate money to the poor.

    C. To sort out the clothes.

    D. To get some summer clothes out.

45. A. He should go to the information center.

    B. He should contact a travel agency.

    C. He should consider a youth hostel.

    D. He should look it up online.

The End

中級聽力測驗錄音稿 script-1

Track01

英語能力分級檢定測驗中級
聽力測驗

本測驗分三部分，全為四選一之選擇題，每部分各 15 題，共 45 題。

第一部分有 15 題，為第 1 題至第 15 題。試題冊上有數幅圖畫，每一圖畫有 1 ～ 3 個描述該圖之題目，每題請聽錄音機播出題目以及 A、B、C、D 四個英語敘述之後，選出與所看到的圖畫最相符的答案，每題只播出一遍。

例：（看）

（聽）What is this?

A. This is a desk.

B. This is a chair.

C. This is a box.

D. This is a bed.

正確答案為 A，請在答案紙上塗黑作答。

Track**02** A、B、C、D 四個句子中，只有句子 A 與圖片內容最相符，因此正確答案應該選 A。請在答案紙上塗黑作答。現在請翻開試題冊。(Pause 4 seconds) 現在開始聽力測驗第一部分。

For questions number 1 and 2, please look at picture A.

Question number 1：

When is the day when there is a full day of dental services?

A. On Saturday.

B. On Friday.

C. On Wednesday.

D. On Monday.

Question number 2：

When is the day when there are no dental services?

A. On Monday.

B. On Sunday.

C. On Saturday.

D. On Friday.

For question number 3 and 4, please look at picture B.

Question number 3：

What is the woman's job most likely to be?

A. Accountant.

B. Designer.

C. Teacher.

D. Salesperson.

Track02

Question number 4：

Look at the clock on the wall. What time is it?

A. 15：05

B. 14：45

C. 14：55

D. 14：50

For question number 5 and 6, please look at picture C.

Question number 5：

Which one is most expensive among the four items?

A. The pen.

B. The tape.

C. The bag.

D. The calculator.

Track**03**

Question number 6：Which one costs the least among the four items?

A. The bag.

B. The tape.

C. The pen.

D. The calculator.

For questions number 7, please look at picture D.

Question number 7：

What are the two children doing?

A. They are doing a bungee jumping.

B. They are riding a hot air balloon.

C. They are taking photos.

D. They are dumping garbage.

For questions number 8 and 9, please look at picture E.

Question number 8：

Look at Wendy. What is she doing?

A. She's lifting weight.

B. She's playing tennis.

C. She's dancing.

D. She's doing yoga.

Question number 9：

What kind of hairstyle does Wendy wear?

Track**03**

A. She wears straight hair.

B. She has curly hair.

C. She has short hair.

D. She had her hair permed.

For questions number 10, please look at picture F.

Question number 10：

What does the map show?

A. The restaurant is across from the hotel.

B. The post office is next to the restaurant.

C. The restaurant is across from the park.

D. The park is next to the MRT entrance.

For question number 11 and 12, please look at picture G.

Question number 11：

What is the man probably doing right now?

A. He is probably singing.

B. He is probably doing a presentation.

C. He is probably doing the lighting.

D. He is probably cleaning.

Track**04**

Question number 12：What kind of graph is he showing?

A. Pie chart.

B. Bar chart.

C. Image chart.

D. Line graph.

For question number 13, please look at picture H.

Question number 13：

What is the girl doing at the moment?

A. She is singing karaoke.

B. She is reading a book.

C. She is listening to music.

D. She is talking on the phone.

For question number 14 and 15, please look at picture I.

Question number 14：

A department store is announcing a special sale.

When will the special sale take place?

A. The special sale will start from March 10, 2013.

B. The special sale will start from October 13, 2013.

C. The special sale will start from October 30, 2013.

D. The special sale will start from October 31, 2013.

Track**04**

Question number 15：

Which of the following information is true?

A. There will be a special discount on maternity clothing.

B. Children clothes will be completely 70% off.

C. The prices of kids wear will be reduced by as much as 30%.

D. A discount will be given to those who buy more than 3 items.

　　第二部分有 15 題，為第 16 題至第 30 題。每題請聽錄音機播出一英語問句或直述句之後，從試題冊上 A、B、C、D 四個回答或回應中，找出一個最適合的作答。每題只播出一遍。

　　請聽例題：Where is your brother now?

A. He's 20 years old.

B. He's a doctor.

C. He's thirsty.

D. He's in New York.

　　A、B、C、D 四個回答中，只有 D 是正確回答，因此正確答案應該選 D。現在開始聽力測驗第二部分。

Track**05**

16. How are you doing?

17. What did you do last weekend?

18. How often do you go out for dinner?

19. Have you tried the buffet in that hotel?

20. What are your hobbies?

21. Have you ever been to the Taipei Zoo before?

22. Sorry, my boss is not available now. Would you like to leave a message?

23. What time is this post office closed on weekdays?

24. What are you going to do this summer?

25. How often do you exercise?

26. Excuse me. Is there a toilet inside this convenient store?

27. How do you usually go to school every day?

Track05

28. Do you know what to major in in college?

29. Why do you want to learn English?

30. You should take a break! You have been studying for about 2 hours.

第三部分有 15 題，為第 31 題至第 45 題。每題請聽錄音機播出一段對話及一個相關的問題後，從試題冊上 A、B、C、D 四個備選答案中找出一個最適合的回答。每段對話及問題只播出一遍。

請聽例題：(Man) How do you go to school every day?

(Woman) Usually on foot. Sometimes by bus.

Question：How does the woman go to school?

A. She always walks to school.
B. She usually takes a bus.

C. She either walks or takes a bus.

D. She usually goes on foot,never by bus.

　　A、B、C、D 四個備選答案中，只有 C 是正確回答，因此正確答案應該選 C。現在開始聽力測驗第三部分。

Track06

31. W：Do you know we'll have a new English teacher?

　　M：Yes. People say he gives a lot of homework.

　　W：Besides,he gives many tests.

　　M：We will have a hard time.

Q： According to the speakers, which following statement is true about the new teacher?

32. M：How can I help you?

　　W：I'd like to send this parcel to Japan.

　　M：Do you want to send it as registered mail?

　　W：Yes, that would suit me.

Q： What place does the man probably work in?

33. W：Have you tried English learning magazines?

    M：I tried it before,but I was too lazy to listen totheir programs.

    W： Some magazines also come with MP3.

    M： I am too lazy to listen to MP3,too.

    W： If so,how can you pass "listening comprehension"?

    M： You are right. No wonder I always get low points.

Track**06**

Q： What are the two people talking about?

34. M：Do you know you can apply for the scholarship?

    W：Me? I don't think I did that well last semester.

    M：It is a scholarship especially for those who got high scores in English.

    W： Really? Thank you for telling me.

    M： Didn't you win the English writing competition? You must put that in!

Q： Why can the female student apply for scholarship?

35. W：When do you learn English vocabulary?

    M：Every morning after I get up,and you?

    W：Whenever I find time,I try to learn English vocabulary.

M：For me, my brain seems to work best in the early morning.

W：I see. Next time I'll try to memorize new words in the morning, too.

Q：Why does the man like to learn vocabulary in the early morning?

Track**07**

36. W：Do you know Susan is in a hospital?

　　M：That's too bad. What happened?

　　W：She was hit by a motorcycle yesterday.

　　M：Should we visit her together this afternoon?

　　W：Sure. What should we bring with us?

　　M：Some flowers might do.

Q：Why is Susan in a hospital now?

37. W：I hear you just got a promotion.

　　M：How did you know that?

　　W：A little bird told me.

　　M：Well, it's true. I can treat you to dinner this Friday.

Q： How did the woman know about the man's promotion?

Track**07**

38. M： Where have you been since you arrive in Taiwan?

W： Let me see⋯The Taipei 101, Sun Yat-san Memorial Hall, Tam Shui and so on.

M： Will you be going to the Palace Museum?

W： Yes, tomorrow.

M： A visit to that Museum is a must in Taiwan.

Q： What does the man think the woman should do in Taiwan?

39. M： I'm sorry to hear your mother passed away the day before yesterday.

W： It happened so sudden.

M： Maybe you could take a day off? Your teacher would understand it.

W： Thank you, but I really don't want to miss any class.

M： Your mother must be very proud of such a good daughter.

Q： What does the man think the female student could do?

40. M： Do you have a moment? I'd like to talk to you in private.

W： Of course. What's the matter?

M： We'd like to buy a cake for Ms. Huang for her birthday.

W： That's great. How much should I pay for it?

M： If you could buy the cake and bring it to the office, you wouldn't have to pay.

W： It's a deal.

Q： **What does the woman mean?**

Track**08**

41. W： How did you lose so much weight this summer?

M： I went to a gym almost every day,and I had a personal trainer.

W： How about eating?

M： Yes, my personal trainer watched over my diet, too.

Q： **How did the man successfully lose weight?**

42. M： How much time do you have to do this assignment?

W： One more month. Could you give me a hand?

M： Hang on—you are supposed to work on this project on your own.

W： Oh, I know what you mean. Please just please give me some directions.

Track**08**

Q：**What is the man afraid that the woman might do?**

43. M：What do you want to be in the future?

    W：I'd really like to be a great journalist.

    M：Of course, you can. You can major in Journalism in college.

    W：Are you serious? Do you really think I can make it?

Q：**What does the man think of the woman's dream?**

44. W：Don't you think we should donate some old clothes to the poor people?

    M：Of course. Winter is coming, and some people probably don't have proper clothes.

    W：First, we should select what clothes to give them.

    M：You are right. Maybe the clothes that can keep them warm.

    W：Good thinking. So, let's start!

Q：**What will the two people probably do next?**

Track**08**

45. M： Do you know any good hotels in this area?

W： Of course. What is your price range?

M： In fact, I have no idea about the reasonable price.

W： I suggest you do a bit of research on the Internet.

M： That's a good idea. There must be a wide range of accommodation there.

Q： **What does the woman think the man should do?**

This is the end of the Listening Comprehension Test.

第一回聽力模擬試題
解答與翻譯

GEPT 中級聽力測驗（LTI-A）解答

1.D	11.B	21.B	31.C	41.C
2.B	12.B	22.C	32.C	42.B
3.C	13.C	23.D	33.C	43.A
4.C	14.D	24.B	34.D	44.C
5.C	15.C	25.D	35.A	45.D
6.B	16.B	26.C	36.C	
7.B	17.D	27.B	37.D	
8.A	18.B	28.D	38.B	
9.A	19.A	29.A	39.B	
10.C	20.C	30.D	40.A	

中級 Listening Comprehension & Speaking

NEW

新制全民英檢

GEPT

The General English Proficiency Test [Intermediate]

聽力&口說 模擬試題+解答

英語能力分級檢定測驗中級

模擬試題第一回

聽力測驗

　　本測驗分三部分，全為四選一之選擇題，每部分各 15 題，共 45 題。

　　第一部分有 15 題，為第 1 題至第 15 題。試題冊上有數幅圖畫，每一圖畫有 1 ～ 3 個描述該圖之題目，每題請聽錄音機播出題目以及 A、B、C、D 四個英語敍述之後，選出與所看到的圖畫最相符的答案，每題只播出一遍。

☆第 1 至 2 題請看 A 圖

1. 哪一天有全天的牙醫服務？
A. 星期六
B. 星期五
C. 星期三
D. 星期一

2. 哪一天沒有牙醫服務？
A. 星期一
B. 星期日

C. 星期六

D. 星期五

☆第 3 至 4 題請看 B 圖

3. 這女子的工作最可能是什麼？

A. 會計師

B. 設計師

C. 老師

D. 推銷員

4. 請看牆上的時鐘，現在幾點？

A. 下午三點五分

B. 下午兩點四十五分

C. 下午兩點五十五分

D. 下午兩點五十分

☆第 5 至 6 題請看 C 圖

5. 這四樣東西中哪一樣最昂貴？

A. 筆

B. 膠帶

C. 包包

D. 計算機

6. 這四樣東西中哪一樣最便宜？

A. 包包

B. 膠帶

C. 筆

D. 計算機

☆第 7 題請看 D 圖

7. 這兩個小孩正在做什麼？

A. 他們正在高空彈跳

B. 他們正在乘坐熱氣球

C. 他們正在照相

D. 他們正在丟垃圾

☆第 8 至 9 題請看 E 圖

8. 看看溫蒂，她正在做什麼？

A. 她正在舉重

B. 她正在打網球

C. 她正在跳舞

D. 她正在做瑜珈

9. 溫蒂的髮型是什麼樣式的？

A. 她的髮型為直髮

B. 她的髮型為捲髮

C. 她的髮型為短髮

D. 她燙了頭髮

☆第 10 題請看 F 圖

10. 這張地圖告訴我們什麼訊息？

A. 餐廳在旅館的對面

B. 郵局在餐廳的旁邊

C. 餐廳在公園的對面

D. 公園在捷運入口的旁邊

☆第 11 至 12 題請看 G 圖

11. 這位男士現在可能正在做什麼？

A. 他可能正在唱歌

B. 他可能正在做簡報

中級 Listening Comprehension & Speaking
NEW
新制全民英檢
GEPT
The General English Proficiency Test [Intermediate]
聽力&口說 模擬試題 +解答

C. 他可能正在處理燈光

D. 他可能正在清掃

12. 他正在展示什麼樣的圖表？

A. 圓餅圖

B. 長條圖

C. 圖像

D. 線狀圖

☆第 13 題請看 H 圖

13. 這個女孩正在做什麼？

A. 她正在唱卡拉 OK

B. 她正在讀書

C. 她正在聽音樂

D. 她正在講電話

☆第 14 至 15 題請看 I 圖

14. 某家百貨公司宣布舉辦特價活動。這個特價活動將於何時開
始？

A. 這個特價活動 2013 年 3 月 10 日開始

B. 這個特價活動 2013 年 10 月 13 日開始

C. 這個特價活動 2013 年 10 月 30 日開始

D. 這個特價活動 2013 年 10 月 31 日開始

15. 下列何者為真？

A. 孕婦裝在特價

B. 童裝全面三折

C. 童裝七折起

D. 購買超過三件有特別優惠

第二部分有 15 題，為第 16 題至第 30 題。每題請聽錄音機播出一英語問句或直述句之後，從試題冊上 A、B、C、D 四個回答或回應中，找出一個最適合的作答。每題只播出一遍。

16. 你還好嗎？

A. 我在做功課

B. 還好，你呢？

C. 我是為你而做的

D. 我在做運動

17. 你上周末做了什麼？

A. 這個星期很忙

中級 Listening Comprehension & Speaking　NEW
新制全民英檢
GEPT
The General English Proficiency Test [Intermediate]
聽力&口說 模擬試題 +解答

B. 這個周末我沒有時間

C. 周末不要工作過度

D. 我去爬山

18. 你多久到外面吃一次飯？

A. 我來為你做晚飯

B. 一星期大約三次

C. 我和我家人共進晚餐

D. 你要為誰做晚餐？

19. 你吃過那家飯店的自助吃到飽嗎？

A. 還沒有，你呢？

B. 你訂了房間沒？

C. 所有的飯店現在都客滿

D. 我不擅長烹飪

20. 你有什麼興趣？

A. 我替你感到高興

B. 在大廳等我

C. 唱歌和跳舞

D. 他的興趣很不尋常

21. 你去過台北動物園嗎？
A. 去過，我喜歡那裡的海鮮
B. 去過，我喜歡那裡的熊貓
C. 沒去過，我要買隻貓
C. 沒去過，你可以和我的狗玩

22. 不好意思，我的老闆現在沒空，你要留言嗎？
A. 好，請不要讓他失望
B. 不用了，請安撫他
C. 好，請寫下我的電話號碼
D. 不用了，請回我的信

23. 郵局周一至周五什麼時候關門？
A. 我可以帶你參觀這間郵局
B. 我們郵局正忙著關門
C. 你可以在辦公室張貼這張公告
D. 周一至周五下午六點關門

24. 你今年夏天要做什麼？
A. 去年你也出國了嗎？
B. 我要上英語密集課程
C. 去年夏天我去日本

D. 謝謝你邀請我

25. 你多久運動一次？
A. 我在健身中心鍛鍊身體
B. 相較於瑜珈，我比較喜歡太極
C. 我喜歡跳舞
D. 每天大約一小時

26. 不好意思，這家便利商店內有廁所嗎？
A. 你在這裡工作嗎？
B. 有什麼需要我服務的？
C. 有的，在那裡
D. 有的，離這家便利商店不遠

27. 通常你每天怎麼樣上學？
A. 很抱歉我遲到了
B. 通常我騎腳踏車上學
C. 我們的校車又拋錨了
D. 七點半來接我

28. 你上大學想要主修什麼？
A. 我主要的問題是健康

B. 我想要在大學工作

C. 大學太多所了

D. 英國文學

29. 為什麼你想要學英文？

A. 我想要和外國人溝通

B. 對，我真的想要把英文學好

C. 從來沒有，但是我會想要

D. 沒有，我不喜歡學習英文

30. 你應該要休息了！你已經讀書超過兩小時了。

A. 你今年有休假嗎？

B. 讓我為你詳細解說

C. 下個月我會有個短期的假

D. 什麼！已經超過兩小時了！

第三部分：簡短對話，本部分共 15 題，每題請聽錄音機播出一段對話及一個相關的問題後，從試題冊上 A、B、C、D 四個備選答案中找出一個最適合的回答。每段對話及問題只播出一遍。

31.

女：你知道我們會有位新的英文老師嗎？

男：知道，聽説他的功課很多。

女：而且他會考很多試。

男：我們以後的日子不好過了。

問題：根據説話者，下列哪個關於新老師的敘述為真？

A. 他是個數學老師

B. 他規定學生只能用英語説話

C. 他會給學生很多考試和功課

D. 他的個性很差

32.

男：有什麼需要我幫忙的地方嗎？

女：我想要把這個包裹寄到日本。

男：你要寄掛號嗎？

女：要，那就是我想要的。

問題：這個男子可能在哪裡工作？

A. 在銀行裡

B. 在餐廳裡

C. 在郵局裡

D. 在旅行社裡

33.

女：你試過英語學習雜誌嗎？

男：我從前試過，但是我實在懶得聽他們的節目。

女：有些雜誌也有附 MP3。

男：我也懶得聽他們的節目。

女：你這個樣子怎麼能通過聽力測驗？

男：妳說的對，怪不得我的分數總是很低。

問題：這兩個人在討論什麼？

A. 聽廣播新聞

B. 最新的雜誌

C. 改進英文的方法

D. 在網路上聽新聞

34.

男：妳知道妳可以申請獎學金嗎？

女：我？我不認為我上學期的成績有那麼好。

男：這個獎學金是特別頒贈給英語成績優秀的學生。

女：真的？謝謝你告訴我。

男：妳不是得了英文寫作獎嗎？妳一定要把這個寫進去！

問題：為什麼這個女學生可以申請獎學金？

A. 她家境清寒

B. 她從未出國

C. 她來自小村落

D. 她的英文成績很好

35.

女：你什麼時候背英文單字？

男：每天早上起床後，妳呢？

女：只要我有時間，就會儘量背單字。

男：對我而言，我的頭腦似乎在清晨效率最佳。

女：這樣我明白了。下次我也來試試看一大早背單字。

問題：為什麼這個男子喜歡在清晨背單字？

A. 他的頭腦在清晨最清醒

B. 他白天一整天沒時間

C. 他隨時在背單字

D. 他每早都有一個考試

36.

女：你知道素珊現在在醫院嗎？

男：那真不妙。發生了什麼事？

女：昨天她被一輛摩托車撞到了。

男：我們要不要今天下午一起去看她？

女：當然好，我們該帶什麼呢？

男：帶些花應該就可以。

問題：為什麼素珊現在在醫院？

A. 她到那裡去拜訪一個朋友

B. 她到那裡去買些花

C. 她昨天出了車禍

D. 她到那裡去做健康檢查

37.

女：我聽説你剛獲得升職。

男：妳怎麼知道的？

女：有人告訴我。

男：這個倒是真的，這個禮拜五我可以請妳吃晚餐。

問題：這個女子怎麼知道這男子的升職？

A. 她和他一起工作

B. 她已經工作很久了

C. 她很喜歡鳥

D. 她從別人那裡聽到這個消息

38.

男：來台灣後，妳到過什麼地方？

女：讓我想想…台北 101、國父紀念館、淡水等等。

男：妳會去故宮博物院嗎？

女：會，明天。

男：來台灣一定要去那家博物館。

問題：這個男子認為這女子來台灣該做什麼？

A. 她應該要到淡水玩

B. 她應該要參觀故宮博物院

C. 她應該要到台北 101 頂端

D. 她應該要參加台北之旅

39.

男：聽說妳母親前天過世，我深感遺憾。

女：實在太突然了。

男：或許妳可以請一天的假？妳的老師會諒解的。

女：謝謝你，但是我真的不想錯過任何的課。

男：妳的母親一定會以妳這樣好的女兒為榮的。

問題：這個男子認為這個女學生可以怎麼做？

A. 去參加喪禮

B. 一天不要上課

C. 照顧她的母親

D. 到醫院看她的母親

40.

男：妳有時間嗎？我想要私下跟妳談一下。

女：當然，什麼事？

男：我們想要買個生日蛋糕給黃小姐。

女：那樣很好，我該付多少錢？

男：如果妳可以買蛋糕並且帶蛋糕來公司，就不用付錢。

女：那就一言為定。

問題：這個女子的意思是？

A. 她同意負責蛋糕

B. 她會和蛋糕店做個買賣

C. 她不喜歡這個想法

D. 她沒有買蛋糕的錢

41.

女：今年夏天你是如何減重的？

男：我幾乎每天上健身中心，而且我有個私人教練。

女：飲食方面如何？

男：是的，我的私人教練也監控我的飲食。

問題：這個男子是如何成功減重的？

A. 他到某間診所去

B. 他從他的醫師那裡得到處方

C. 他健身而且注意飲食

D. 他沒有注意他的體重

42.

男：妳還有多少時間來完成這個任務？

女：還有一個月。你可以幫我嗎？

男：等一下，妳應該要靠自己來做這個專案。

女：我知道你的意思。請給我一些方向好嗎？

問題：這個男子擔心這女子會怎麼做？

A. 工作過度

B. 太依賴他

C. 向他問路

D. 享受休息時刻

43.

男：妳將來想要做什麼？

女：我真的很想當個優秀的記者。

男：妳當然可以。妳可以在大學主修新聞學。

女：你是認真的嗎？你真的認為我可以做得到？

問題：這個男子認為這女子的夢想怎麼樣？

A. 他認為她能實現夢想

B. 他認為這個女子太愛作夢

C. 他似乎是個算命師

D. 他也想當個記者

44.

女：你覺不覺得我們應該捐點舊衣服給窮人？

男：當然好，冬天就要來了，有些人可能沒有合適的衣服。

女：首先，我們應該選擇要給他們的衣服。

男：妳說的對，或許能夠讓他們保暖的衣物。

女：這個想法很好。那麼我們這就開始！

問題：這兩個人可能接下來會做什麼？

A. 學習如何做衣服

B. 捐錢給窮人

C. 整理衣服

D. 找出夏天的衣物

45.

男：妳知道附近有什麼好旅館嗎？

女：當然，你想付的價錢範圍是？

男：事實上，我對該付的合理價錢沒概念。

女：我建議你上網研究一下。

男：這個主意很好。那裡一定有很多住宿地點可選。

問題：這個女子認為這男子該怎麼做？

A. 他應該去服務台

B. 他應該聯絡旅行社

C. 他應該考慮青年旅館

D. 他應該上網查住宿資料

第二回聽力模擬試題
中級聽力測驗模擬試題 -2

英語能力分級檢定測驗中級

聽力測驗

本測驗分三部分，全為四選一之選擇題，每部分各 15 題，共 45 題。本測驗總分 100 分，平均每題 2.2 分，作答時間約 30 分鐘。

中級 Listening Comprehension & Speaking
NEW
新制全民英檢
GEPT 聽力&口說 模擬試題+解答
The General English Proficiency Test [Intermediate]

第一部分：看圖辨義

　　本部分共 15 題，試題冊上有數幅圖畫，每一圖畫有 1 ～ 3 個描述該圖之題目，每題請聽錄音機播出題目以及 A、B、C、D 四個英語敍述之後，選出與所看到的圖畫最相符的答案，每題只播出一遍。

例：

（看）

（聽）What is this?

　　A. This is a desk.

　　B. This is a chair.

　　C. This is a box.

　　D. This is a bed.

正確答案為 A，請在答案紙上塗黑作答。

第四章

聽力模擬試題

A.

B.

C.

ENGLISH BOOKS
DISCOUNT *Seventh of each month*

Buy 2 and SAVE 30% !

D.

E.

F.

G.

第四章
聽力模擬試題

第二部分：問答

本部分共 15 題，每題請聽錄音機播出一英語問句或直述句之後，從試題冊上 A、B、C、D 四個回答或回應中，找出一個最適合的作答。每題只播出一遍。

例：

（聽）Where is your brother now?

（看）A. He's 20 years old.

B. He's a doctor.

C. He's thirsty.

D. He's in New York.

正確答案為 D，請在答案紙上塗黑作答。

16. A. Did you go to the interview?

B. Nobody wants to interview you.

C. I did my best anyway.

D. Let me interview you.

17. A. I went on a tour around Taiwan.

B. When will the Chinese New Year be this year?

中級 Listening Comprehension & Speaking

NEW

新制全民英檢
GEPT
聽力&口說 模擬試題 +解答

The General English Proficiency Test [Intermediate]

C. I'll visit Japan with my family.

D. The Lunar New Year is similar to Christmas.

18. A. It's too bad that you're going away.

B. That's a good idea!

C. Will you be back soon?

D. Many tourists visited Taiwan last year.

19. A. An English book.

B. A new CD.

C. A cake recipe.

D. A talk show on TV.

20. A. He proposed to you again?

B. Neither do I.

C. You don't know me at all.

D. Don't push me.

21. A. No,I always go there by car.

B. Yes,I like the city very much.

C. No,I went to high school there.

D. I prefer Taipei to Taichung.

22. A. I don't enjoy English classes.

B. English is easy to learn,isn't it?

C. About 10 hours every week.

D. I learned to speak English in 3 months.

23. A. I didn't finish high school.

B. Usually I go home by bus after school.

C. I live very far away from the school.

D. My school finishes at 16：15.

24. A. Excuse me.

B. Thank you.

C. Sorry to hear that.

D. Don't mention it.

25. A. Why? Is there a problem?

B. Please follow me this way.

C. I never like the way he talks.

D. Do you like the way I dress?

26. A. In a 5 star hotel.

B. Bread and orange juice.

C. With my family.

D. Near my school.

27. A. We'll have a new English teacher.

   B. I prefer English to Chinese.

   C. Probably my English teacher.

   D. My English teacher is not patient.

28. A. Chinese typing only.

   B. I enjoy reading and singing.

   C. I don't like my full-time job.

   D. Next year I'll take a month off.

29. A. Sometimes I do,not often.

   B. We had exams last week.

   C. No,the exams are harder than I thought.

   D. Yes,exams cannot help me learn.

30. A. Sometime later.

   B. You can say that again.

   C. No,but I wouldn't want to see one,either.

   D. Yes,you're lucky to know me.

第三部分：簡短對話

本部分共 15 題，每題請聽錄音機播出一段對話及一個相關的問題後，從試題冊上 A、B、C、D 四個備選答案中找出一個最適合的回答。每段對話及問題只播出一遍。

例：（聽）(Man)How do you go to school every day?

(Woman)Usually on foot. Sometimes by bus.

(Question)How does the woman go to school?

（看）A. She always walks to school.

B. She usually takes a bus.

C. She either walks or takes a bus.

D. She usually goes on foot,never by bus.

正確答案為 C，請在答案紙上塗黑作答。

31. A. To make an appointment.

B. To remind him of the due date.

C. To ask him to do her a favor.

D. To ask him to take a break.

32. A. To ask her neighbors.

    B. To get a new dog.

    C. To notify the police.

    D. To write a notice and put it up.

33. A. In a movie theater.

    B. In a clinic.

    C. In a supermarket.

    D. In a restaurant.

34. A. If she should learn a music instrument.

    B. If she should be a music teacher.

    C. What to major in in college.

    D. What music to listen to.

35. A. He cannot get used to Taipei.

    B. He is very used to life in Taipei.

    C. He will move away from Taipei soon.

    D. He does not live in Taipei any more.

36. A. To get a special discount.

    B. To sell them to others.

    C. To collect a series of books.

    D. To have free gift paper wrapping.

37. A. Jazz reminds him of his hometown.

B. Jazz can help him unwind.

C. He played Jazz before.

D. His father is a Jazz player.

38. A. The man never does any housework.

B. She does not like do laundry.

C. The man never pays the bills.

D. She does not like mopping the floor.

39. A. The test is too long.

B. The test is too hard..

C. The time is too short.

D. The questions are not good.

40. A. She does not like practicing Yoga.

B. She seldom goes to Yoga classes.

C. She thinks Yoga is too hard for her.

D. She practices Yoga when she is fit for it.

41. A. He was very pleased with the exams.

B. He didn't have enough time to prepare for the exams.

C. He hopes his hard work is appreciated.

D. He was disappointed with himself.

42. A. To enjoy too many concerts.

    B. To overwork herself on the trip.

    C. To visit her friends over there.

    D. To spend too much time at the beach.

43. A. The man's experiences of working in a café.

    B. The woman's experiences of making coffee.

    C. The man's dream of running a café.

    D. The woman's goal of saving.

44. A. He likes the radio program very much.

    B. He dislikes the radio program.

    C. He finds the radio program too hard.

    D. He missed the radio program for 3 weeks.

45. A. It's out of the question.

    B. It's a good idea.

    C. It costs too much.

    D. It will make a mess.

中級聽力測驗錄音稿 script-2

Track**09**

英語能力分級檢定測驗中級

聽力測驗

　　本測驗分三部分，全為四選一之選擇題，每部分各 15 題，共 45 題。

　　第一部分有 15 題，為第 1 題至第 15 題。試題冊上有數幅圖畫，每一圖畫有 1 ～ 3 個描述該圖之題目，每題請聽錄音機播出題目以及 A、B、C、D 四個英語敘述之後，選出與所看到的圖畫最相符的答案，每題只播出一遍。

　　例：（看）

　　（聽）What is this?

　　　　A. This is a desk.

　　　　B. This is a chair.

　　　　C. This is a box.

　　　　D. This is a bed.

　　正確答案為 A，請在答案紙上塗黑作答。

A、B、C、D 四個句子中，只有句子 A 與圖片內容最相符，因此正確答案應該選 A。請在答案紙上塗黑作答。現在請翻開試題冊。(Pause 4 seconds) 現在開始聽力測驗第一部分。

For questions number 1 and 2, please look at picture A.

Question number 1：

Where are these two people?

A. They're in a school.

B. They're in a coffee shop.

C. They're in a tall building.

D. They're on the road.

Question number 2：

Look at the two people again. Which description matches the picture?

A. The old woman is walking by herself.

B. The old woman is carrying nothing.

C. The schoolgirl is helping the old woman across the road.

D. The schoolgirl is walking across the road alone.

For question number 3 and 4, please look at picture B.

Question number 3：

What is the man probably doing now?

A. He is probably painting.

B. He is probably traveling.

C. He is probably eating.

D. He is probably smoking.

Track10

Question number 4：

Look at the man closely. What is he holding now?

A. A map.

B. A flasher.

C. A camera.

D. A cup.

For question number 5 to 7, please look at picture C.

Question number 5：

To get a discount, when is the best time to buy English books in this bookstore?

A. The 7th of every month.

B. The 3rd of every month.

C. The first week of every month.

D. The third week of every month.

Listening
Comprehension
& Speaking

NEW

中級
新制全民英檢
GEPT 聽力&口說 模擬試題+解答

The General English Proficiency Test [Intermediate]

Track **11**

Question number 6：

What discount can one get if one buys 2 English books during sales?

A. 70% off.

B. 40% off.

C. 30% off.

D. 20% off.

Question number 7：

How much would it cost if one buys 2 copies of 300 Dollar English

books on Dec. 7th?

A. 600.

B. 420.

C. 300.

D. 180.

For questions number 8 to 9, please look at picture D.

Question number 8：

Where is possibly this place?

A. A movie theater.

B. A sports center.

C. A classroom.

D. A park.

Question number 9：

Look at the old man closely. What is he doing?

A. He is reading a newspaper.

B. He is talking to his neighbors.

C. He is walking his dog.

D. He is watering the flowers.

Track 11

For questions number 10 to 11, please look at picture E.

Question number 10：

Which item is the most expensive one here?

A. The alarm clock.

B. The cup.

C. The notebook.

D. The teddy bear.

Question number 11：

Which statement about these items is true?

A. The notebook costs the same as the teddy bear.

B. The teddy bear costs the same as the alarm clock.

C. The alarm clock costs the same as the cup.

D. The cup costs the same as the notebook.

Track 12

For questions number 12 and 13, please look at picture F.

Question number 12：

Look at the picture. Which description matches the picture?

A. They are listening to a concert.

B. They are having a class.

C. They are having lunch together.

D. They are playing Hide and Seek.

Question number 13：

What does the man in the middle probably do for a living?

A. Priest.

B. Programmer.

C. Talk show host.

D. Teacher.

For question number 14 and 15, please look at picture G.

Question number 14：

What is the girl doing there?

A. She is cleaning up the park.

B. She is painting a picture.

C. She is talking on the phone.

D. She is exercising in the park.

Question number 15：

What is the weather like in the picture?

A. It is raining.

B. It is cloudy.

Track **12**

C. It is sunny.

D. It is snowing.

第二部分有 15 題，為第 16 題至第 30 題。每題請聽錄音機播出一英語問句或直述句之後，從試題冊上 A、B、C、D 四個回答或回應中，找出一個最適合的作答。每題只播出一遍。

請聽例題：Where is your brother now?

A. He's 20 years old.

B. He's a doctor.

C. He's thirsty.

D. He's in New York.

A、B、C、D 四個回答中，只有 D 是正確回答，因此正確答案應該選 D。現在開始聽力測驗第二部分。

16. How did your interview go yesterday?

17. Where did you spend your Lunar New Year's holidays?

18. Let's go to Taitung during this winter vacation.

19. What are you watching now?

20. I just have this feeling that his proposal won't work.

21. Have you been to Taichung before?

22. How many hours of English classes do you have in a week?

23. When does your school finish every day?

24. Your report is really well-done.

25. Are you sure you are going to do it this way?

26. What did you have breakfast this morning?

27. Who is your favorite teacher in school?

28. What kinds of part-time jobs have you done before?

29. Do you get nervous in exams?

Track**13**

30. Have you seen a car accident somewhere?

第三部分有 15 題，為第 31 題至第 45 題。每題請聽錄音機播出一段對話及一個相關的問題後，從試題冊上 A、B、C、D 四個備選答案中找出一個最適合的回答。每段對話及問題只播出一遍。

請聽例題：(Man) How do you go to school every day?
(Woman) Usually on foot. Sometimes by bus.

Question：How does the woman go to school?

A. She always walks to school.

B. She usually takes a bus.

C. She either walks or takes a bus.

D. She usually goes on foot,never by bus.

A、B、C、D 四個備選答案中，只有 C 是正確回答，因此正確答案應該選 C。現在開始聽力測驗第三部分。

Track**14**

31. W： When do you have to hand in your homework?

　　M： In a week.

　　W： Aren't you afraid you won't be able to meet the deadline?

　　M： No, I already finished it the day before yesterday.

Q： Why does the woman ask the man the questions about homework?

32. M： Why do you look so upset?

　　W： My dog ran away the day before yesterday.

　　M： Have you looked for it in the neighborhood?

　　W： Yes, but I couldn't find it.

　　M： Then, you should put up a notice to look for it.

　　W： That sounds like a good idea. I'll do it right away.

Q： What is the woman going to do next?

33. W： What seems to be the problem?

　　M： I have a serious headache and a sore throat.

　　W： Let me see…

　　M： Yesterday I had a cold shower, and I seemed to catch a cold.

W： Take the medicine three times a day after meals.

M： Thank you.

Track**14**

Q： Where does this conversation probably take place?

34. M： Do you want to learn a music instrument?

W： Not really. I don't have a lot of time after school.

M： Don't you want to learn to play the piano?

W： Not at all. I am happy to just listen to the piano music.

Q： What are the two people talking about?

35. W： How old were you when you moved to Taipei?

M： About 10 years old.

W： Did you attend high school in Taipei?

M： Yes,both junior and senior high schools.

W： How do you like Taipei?

M： I am used to living in Taipei,and I consider it my second hometown.

Q： What does the man think of Taipei?

Track**15**

36. W： Why did you buy so many books?

M： They have a special sale in the bookstore, and you get 30% off if you buy 5 books.

W： I see. I am going to see when you have the time to read all of the 5 books.

M： Don't worry. I'm going to give some of them away as gifts.

Q： Why did the man buy so many books at one time?

37. W： What kinds of music do you like?

M： I enjoy listening to Jazz.

W： Why?

M： It helps me relax before going to bed.

Q： Why does the man enjoy listening to Jazz?

38. W： I've been doing all the house chores, and you've never done anything.

M： That's not true. Last night I dumped the garbage.

W： From now on,you should at least do the laundry and mop the floor.

M： All right. I will.

第四章
聽力模擬試題

Q： What is the woman complaining about?

39. M： Why didn't you pass your English test?

Track **15**

   W： The test is too difficult.

   M： How can you be so sure?

   W： Everybody said so.

   M： Make more effort to learn English, will you?

Q： What does the female student think of the English test?

40. M： Where do you practice yoga?

   W： In a sports center.

   M： How often do you attend your yoga lessons there?

   W： It really depends on my physical condition.

Q： What does the woman mean?

41. W： How did you do in your final exams?

   M： All I can say is that I did my best.

   W： Good. That is the best answer I'd like to hear.

   M： Well, if I had had more time,I would have studied harder.

Q： What was the male student trying to say?

Track**16**

42. M： I hear you are going on a business trip in Sydney.

W： Yes,I'm really looking forward to the world class beaches there.

M： Hold on. Do you really think you'll have the time to enjoy the beaches there?

W： Maybe one afternoon?

Q： What is the man afraid that the woman might do?

43. M： I'd really like to run a café if I could.

W： Well, that does not sound too difficult. Have you learned how to make coffee before?

M： Yes, I did, but it was not very professional.

W： That's a good start. At least you had some experiences of cooking coffee.

M： Thank you for encouraging me.

Q： What are the two people talking about?

44. W： What radio program are you listening to now?

M： It's a new English learning radio program, called "I love English."

W： How do you like it?

M： So far I have been a faithful listener for 3 weeks, and I don't want to miss it any day.

W： Sounds amazing. You haven't been listening to any English learning radio program for that long.

Track **16**

Q： What is the man's opinion of the radio program?

45. M： Do you think we can host an American backpacker next month?

W： Are you kidding? Where are you going to let this guest sleep?

M： Well, on the couch in the living room.

W： The answer is no.

M： Well, I'll have to ask the backpacker to stay in a youth hostel then.

Q： What does the woman think about the man's suggestion?

This is the end of the Listening Comprehension Test.

中級 Listening Comprehension & Speaking

NEW

新制全民英檢

GEPT

The General English Proficiency Test [Intermediate]

聽力&口說 模擬試題 +解答

第二回聽力模擬試題 解答與翻譯

GEPT 中級聽力測驗 (LTI-A) 解答

1.D	11.C	21.B	31.B	41.B
2.C	12.B	22.C	32.D	42.D
3.B	13.D	23.D	33.B	43.C
4.C	14.B	24.B	34.A	44.A
5.A	15.C	25.A	35.B	45.A
6.C	16.C	26.B	36.A	
7.B	17.A	27.C	37.B	
8.D	18.B	28.A	38.A	
9.C	19.D	29.A	39.B	
10.D	20.B	30.C	40.D	

第四章

聽力模擬試題

英語能力分級檢定測驗中級
模擬試題第二回
聽力測驗

本測驗分三部分,全為四選一之選擇題,每部分各 15 題,共 45
題。

第一部分有 15 題,為第 1 題至第 15 題。試題冊上有數幅圖畫,
每一圖畫有 1 ～ 3 個描述該圖之題目,每題請聽錄音機播出題目以及
A、B、C、D 四個英語敘述之後,選出與所看到的圖畫最相符的答案,
每題只播出一遍。

☆第 1 至 2 題請看 A 圖

1. 這兩個人位於何處?
A. 他們在學校裡
B. 他們在咖啡屋裡
C. 他們在高大建築物裡
D. 他們在馬路上

2. 再看這兩個人一次,哪一段描述與圖相符合?
A. 這位老婦人正在獨自行走
B. 這位老婦人手上沒有任何東西

中級 Listening Comprehension & Speaking

NEW

新制全民英檢

GEPT

The General English Proficiency Test [Intermediate]

聽力&口說 模擬試題+解答

C. 女學生正在攙扶這位老婦人過馬路

D. 女學生正在獨自過馬路

☆第 3 至 4 題請看 B 圖

3. 這男子現在可能正在做什麼？

A. 他可能正在畫畫

B. 他可能正在旅遊

C. 他可能正在吃東西

D. 他可能正在抽菸

4. 再仔細看看這男子，他手上拿著什麼？

A. 地圖

B. 手電筒

C. 照相機

D. 茶杯

☆第 5 至 7 題請看 C 圖

5. 什麼時候是在這家書店買英文書的特價期？

A. 每月的七日

B. 每月的三日

C. 每月的第一個星期

D. 每月的第三個星期

6. 如果於特價期間買兩本英文書，可以得到什麼樣的折扣？

A. 三折

B. 六折

C. 七折

D. 八折

7. 如果某人於 12 月 7 日買兩本三百元的英文書，該要付多少錢？

A. 600 元

B. 420 元

C. 300 元

D. 180 元

 ☆第 8 至 9 題請看 D 圖

8. 這個地方可能是何處？

A. 電影院

B. 運動中心

C. 教室

D. 公園

中級 Listening Comprehension & Speaking
新制全民英檢
GEPT NEW 聽力&口說 模擬試題 +解答
The General English Proficiency Test [Intermediate]

9. 仔細看看這個男子，他正在做什麼？

A. 他正在看報紙

B. 他正在和他的鄰居説話

C. 他正在遛狗

D. 他正在澆花

☆第 10 至 11 題請看 E 圖

10. 下列物品哪一樣最昂貴？

A. 鬧鐘

B. 茶杯

C. 筆記本

D. 泰迪熊

11. 下列關於這些物品的敘述何者為真？

A. 筆記本和泰迪熊價錢相同

B. 泰迪熊和鬧鐘價錢相同

C. 鬧鐘和茶杯價錢相同

D. 茶杯和筆記本價錢相同

☆第 12 至 13 題請看 F 圖

12. 看看這張圖片，哪一個敘述與圖相符合？

A. 他們正在聽音樂會

B. 他們正在上課

C. 他們正在一起吃午餐

D. 他們正在玩捉迷藏

13. 在中間的男子可能從事什麼工作？

A. 牧師

B. 程式設計師

C. 脫口秀主持人

D. 老師

☆第 14 至 15 題請看 G 圖

14. 這個女孩正在做什麼？

A. 她正在清掃公園

B. 她正在畫圖

C. 她正在講電話

D. 她正在公園運動

15. 圖中天氣看起來怎麼樣？

A. 在下雨

B. 多雲

C. 天氣晴朗

D. 在下雪

第二部分有 15 題，為第 16 題至第 30 題。每題請聽錄音機播出一英語問句或直述句之後，從試題冊上 A、B、C、D 四個回答或回應中，找出一個最適合的作答。每題只播出一遍。

16. 你昨天的面試如何？

A. 你去參加面試了？

B. 沒有人想訪問你

C. 總之我盡力了

D. 讓我來訪問你

17. 你農曆新年是怎麼過的？

A. 我去環島了

B. 今年農曆新年是什麼時候？

C. 我會和我家人到日本觀光

D. 農曆新年和聖誕節相似

18. 這個寒假我們一起去台東！

A. 真可惜你要走

B. 這個主意很好！

C. 你會回來嗎？

D. 去年來台的觀光客很多

19. 你在看什麼？

A. 一本英文書

B. 一張新 CD

C. 一個蛋糕食譜

D. 電視上的脫口秀

20. 我覺得他的提案不會成功。

A. 他再度向你求婚了？

B. 我也認為不會成功

C. 你一點也不了解我

D. 不要逼我

21. 你到過台中嗎？

A. 沒去過，我總是開車去那裡

B. 去過，我很喜歡那個城市

C. 沒去過，我高中是在那裡唸的

D. 相較於台中，我比較喜歡台北

22. 你一個星期有幾堂英文課？

A. 我不喜歡英文課

B. 英文很容易學，不是嗎？

C. 一星期約十小時

D. 我在三個月內學會説英文

23. 你幾點放學？

A. 我沒唸完高中

B. 放學後我通常搭公車回家

C. 我住的地方離學校很遠

D. 我下午四點十五分放學

24. 你的報告做得很好。

A. 不好意思

B. 謝謝

C. 聽到這個我感到很遺憾

D. 沒關係

25. 你確定要這麼做嗎？

A. 你為什麼這麼問？有問題嗎？

B. 請跟我來這裡

C. 我一直很不喜歡他説話的方式

D. 你覺得我時尚品味如何？

26. 你今天早餐吃了什麼？
A. 在一個五星級的飯店
B. 麵包和柳橙汁
C. 和我的家人
D. 靠近我的學校

27. 在學校你最喜歡哪一位老師？
A. 我們會有位新的英文老師
B. 相較於中文，我比較喜歡英文
C. 或許是我的英文老師
D. 我的英文老師沒有耐心

28. 你從前打過哪種工？
A. 中文打字而已
B. 我喜歡閱讀和唱歌
C. 我不喜歡我的正職
D. 明年我要休一個月的假

29. 你考試的時候會緊張嗎？
A. 有時候會，不是很經常

B. 上星期我們有考試

C. 不會，考試比我預料的還難

D. 會，考試不能幫助我學習

30. 你在哪邊看過車禍嗎？

A. 等一會兒

B. 你說的很有道理

C. 沒看過，不過我也不想看到

D. 看過，認識我你很幸運

第三部分：簡短對話，本部分共 15 題，每題請聽錄音機播出一段對話及一個相關的問題後，從試題冊上 A、B、C、D 四個備選答案中找出一個最適合的回答。每段對話及問題只播出一遍。

31.

女：你什麼時候需要交功課？

男：再過一星期。

女：你難道不怕沒辦法準時交嗎？

男：不怕，昨天我已經做完功課了。

問題：這個女子為什麼問那男生有關功課的事？

A. 和他約定時間碰面

B. 提醒他要交功課的日期
C. 請他幫她個忙
D. 要他休息

32.

男：妳為什麼看起來這麼難過？

女：我的狗昨天跑掉了

男：妳找過附近的地方嗎？

女：找過，可是沒找到。

男：那麼妳該貼張尋狗告示來找狗。

女：這個主意聽起來很好，我馬上就這麼做。

問題：這個女子接下來要做什麼？

A. 問她的鄰居
B. 買隻新狗
C. 通知警局
D. 寫張告示並且張貼起來

33.

女：看起來有什麼問題？

男：我有嚴重的頭痛和喉嚨發炎。

女：讓我看看…

中級 Listening Comprehension & Speaking
NEW
新制全民英檢
GEPT 聽力&口說 模擬試題+解答
The General English Proficiency Test [Intermediate]

男：昨天我洗了個冷水澡，好像感冒了。

女：飯後吃這個藥，一天三次。

男：謝謝。

問題：這段對話可能在哪裡發生？

A. 在一家電影院

B. 在一家診所

C. 在一家超級市場

D. 在一家餐廳

34.

男：妳想要學樂器嗎？

女：不太想，我放學後沒有太多時間。

男：妳不是想學鋼琴嗎？

女：一點也不想。我聽你彈就很高興了。

問題：這兩個人在談什麼？

A. 她是否該學個樂器

B. 她是否要當音樂老師

C. 在大學要主修什麼

D. 該聽什麼音樂。

35.

女：你幾歲搬來台北的？

男：大約十歲。

女：你是在台北唸高中的嗎？

男：對，國中和高中。

女：你喜歡台北嗎？

男：我習慣台北的生活，我把台北當作我第二個家鄉。

問題：這個男子覺得台北怎麼樣？

A. 他無法習慣台北的生活

B. 他很習慣台北的生活

C. 他很快就要搬離台北

D. 他已不再住在台北

36.

女：你為什麼買這麼多的書？

男：書店有特價，買五本就打七折。

女：我明白了。現在我要看你什麼時候有辦法讀完所有這五本書。

男：別煩惱，我會把幾本送給別人當禮物。

問題：這個男子為什麼一次買這麼多本書？

A. 為了獲得折扣

中級
Listening
Comprehension
& Speaking
NEW
新制全民英檢
GEPT
The General English Proficiency Test [Intermediate]
聽力&口說 模擬試題 +解答

B. 為了賣給別人

C. 為了收集一系列的書

D. 為了可以有免費禮物包裝服務

37.

女：你喜歡什麼樣的音樂？

男：我喜歡爵士樂。

女：為什麼？

男：爵士樂幫助我在入睡前放鬆。

問題：為什麼這個男子喜歡爵士樂？

A. 爵士樂讓他想起他的家鄉

B. 爵士樂可以讓他放鬆

C. 他從前玩過爵士樂

D. 他的父親是個爵士樂玩家

38.

女：一直都是我在做所有的家務事，而你一點也沒做。

男：才不是那樣。昨天是我丟垃圾的。

女：從現在開始，至少你要洗衣服和拖地。

男：好吧。

問題：這個女子在抱怨什麼？

A. 這個男子從來不做家事。

B. 她不喜歡洗衣服。

C. 這個男子從來不付帳單的錢

D. 她不喜歡拖地。

39.

男：妳為什麼英文考試不及格？

女：這個測驗太難了。

男：妳怎麼能如此確定？

女：每個人都這麼説。

男：多下些功夫學英文好嗎？

問題：這個女學生覺得這個英文測驗怎麼樣？

A. 這個測驗太長

B. 這個測驗太難

C. 時間太短

D. 問題欠佳

40.

男：妳在哪裡練習瑜珈？

女：在運動中心內。

男：妳一星期上幾次的瑜珈課？

女：依照我的體能來決定

問題：這個女子的意思是？

A. 她不喜歡練習瑜珈

B. 她很少去上瑜珈

C. 她覺得瑜珈對她來說太難

D. 她覺得體能合適時就練瑜珈

41.

女：你的期末考考得怎麼樣？

男：我只能説我盡力了。

女：很好，那就是我最想聽到的答案。

男：如果我有多一點時間的話，我會更用功些。

問題：這個男學生想要説什麼？

A. 他對考試結果很滿意

B. 他沒有充裕的時間來準備考試

C. 他希望能有人讚賞他所下的工夫。

D. 他對自己非常失望。

42.

男：我聽說妳要去雪梨出差。

女：對，我真渴望看到那裡的一流海灘。

男：等一下，妳真的認為妳有時間享受那邊的海灘？

女：或許一個下午？

問題：這個男子擔心這女子可能會做什麼？

A. 享受太多場音樂會

B. 在旅途中工作過度

C. 拜訪她在那邊的朋友

D. 在海灘上花太多的時間

43.

男：如果可以的話，我真想開家咖啡屋。

女：那聽起來不太難。你學過如何煮咖啡嗎？

男：我學過，但是不太專業。

女：那是個好開始，至少你有煮咖啡的經驗。

男：謝謝妳的鼓勵。

問題：這兩個人在討論什麼？

A. 這個男子在咖啡屋工作的經驗

B. 這個女子煮咖啡的經驗

C. 這個男子經驗咖啡屋的夢想

D. 這個女子的存錢目標

44.

女：你現在在聽什麼廣播節目？

男：是一個新的英語廣播教學節目，叫「我愛英語」。

女：你喜歡嗎？

男：到現在我當了三個星期的忠實觀眾，而且我不想錯過任何一次。

女：聽起來真不可思議，你從來沒有聽過那麼久的英語廣播教學節目。

問題：這個男子覺得這個廣播節目怎麼樣？

A. 他很喜歡這個廣播節目

B. 他很不喜歡這個廣播節目

C. 他覺得這個廣播節目太難了

D. 他錯過了這個廣播節目有三星期了

45.

男：妳覺得下個月我們可以招待一個美國背包客嗎？

女：你在開玩笑嗎？你要這個客人睡哪裡？

男：客廳的沙發上。

女：我不同意。

第四章

聽力模擬試題

男：那麼我只能讓這個背包客住青年旅館了。

問題：這個女子覺得這男子的建議怎麼樣？

A. 完全不可行

B. 是個好主意

C. 花費太高

D. 會弄得亂七八糟

中級 Listening Comprehension & Speaking
NEW
新制全民英檢
GEPT
The General English Proficiency Test [Intermediate]
聽力&口說 模擬試題+解答

第三回聽力模擬試題
中級聽力測驗模擬試題 -3

英語能力分級檢定測驗中級

聽力測驗

　　本測驗分三部分，全為四選一之選擇題，每部分各 15 題，共 45 題。本測驗總分 100 分，平均每題 2.2 分，作答時間約 30 分鐘。

第一部分：看圖辨義

　　本部分共 15 題，試題冊上有數幅圖畫，每一圖畫有 1 ～ 3 個描述該圖之題目，每題請聽錄音機播出題目以及 A、B、C、D 四個英語敘述之後，選出與所看到的圖畫最相符的答案，每題只播出一遍。

　　例：

　　（看）

　　（聽）What is this?

　　　　A. This is a desk.

　　　　B. This is a chair.

　　　　C. This is a box.

　　　　D. This is a bed.

正確答案為 A，請在答案紙上塗黑作答。

中級 Listening Comprehension & Speaking

NEW

新制全民英檢

GEPT

The General English Proficiency Test [Intermediate]

聽力&口說 模擬試題 +解答

A.

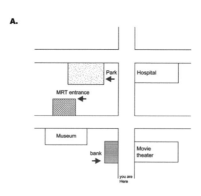

B.

C.

D.

E.

F.

中級 Listening Comprehension & Speaking
NEW
新制全民英檢
GEPT
The General English Proficiency Test [Intermediate]
聽力&口說 模擬試題 +解答

G.

The Opening Times of the Sunshine Clinic

	MON	TUE	WED	THU	FRI	SAT	SUN
morning	V	V	V	V			V
afternoon	V	V	V	V	V	V	V
evening	V	V	V	V	V	V	

V : open

H.

I.

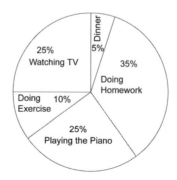

25%
Watching TV

Dinner
5%

35%
Doing
Homework

Doing 10%
Exercise

25%
Playing the Piano

第二部分：問答

　　本部分共 15 題，每題請聽錄音機播出一英語問句或直述句之後，從試題冊上 A、B、C、D 四個回答或回應中，找出一個最適合的作答。每題只播出一遍。

例：

（聽）Where is your brother now?

（看）

　　A. He's 20 years old.

　　B. He's a doctor.

　　C. He's thirsty.

　　D. He's in New York.

正確答案為 D，請在答案紙上塗黑作答。

16. A. I woke up too late again.

　　B. I did my homework,didn't I?

　　C. Usually by bus,sometimes by foot.

　　D. On rainy days,I took a taxi to get to school.

17. A. I am doing all right,and you?

　　B. Recently,I've been quite lazy.

C. I spent lots of time in southern Taiwan.

D. How have you been recently?

18. A. We'll always remember Mr. Chen.

B. I'll see him off at the airport..

C. Are you going to invite Mr. Chen?

D. Yeah,that's a great idea.

19. A. To give a speech.

B. The purple dress,I think.

C. In the conference room.

D. When will the party start?

20. A. In a sports center.

B. That Yoga outfit suits me.

C. That's a good choice.

D. Yes,Yoga helps me a lot.

21. A. I'd like to write a book.

B. I've been to England twice.

C. I don't write in English.

D. No,I haven't read it.

22. A. It's ok. You cannot come here again.

B. We don't have that kind of drink here.

C. All right. What kind of drink would you like?

D. It's okay. Don't be late again.

23. A. Do you want to close your bank account?

B. It's close to the train station.

C. At 15：30 on weekdays.

D. Monday to Friday.

24. A. Chinese is much harder than English.

B. English afternoon tea is my favorite.

C. Where do you learn English?

D. Thank you. I haven't noticed that.

25. A. I've never heard of Facebook.

B. Who introduced you to the Internet?

C. I cannot afford to have Facebook.

D. I have to. All my friends use Facebook.

26. A. She is going to have a big party to celebrate it.

B. Her mother will bake a huge cake for her.

C. Can you tell her I won't be there?

D. Something you make by yourself would be nice.

27. A. We can do it again.

    B. I'll let you know it later.

    C. Sorry,I won't make this mistake again.

    D. You can tell me about it again.

28. A. Yes,I'll apply for that job.

    B. No,I don't like his character.

    C. Maybe as a waitress.

    D. My job has kept me busy.

29. A. Sure,is this gift wrapping paper all right?

    B. This is not our business.

    C. No,it is not for sale.

    D. No,all items bought cannot be refunded.

30. A. Yes,that's really a sad news.

    B. No,I don't like that new teacher.

    C. Yes,I like to experience something new.

    D. No,nobody likes that news.

第三部分：簡短對話

　　本部分共 15 題，每題請聽錄音機播出一段對話及一個相關的問題後，從試題冊上 A、B、C、D 四個備選答案中找出一個最適合的回答。每段對話及問題只播出一遍。

例：〔聽〕(Man) How do you go to school every day?

　　　　　　(Woman) Usually on foot. Sometimes by bus.

(Question)How does the woman go to school?

〔看〕A. She always walks to school.

　　　B. She usually takes a bus.

　　　C. She either walks or takes a bus.

　　　D. She usually goes on foot,never by bus.

正確答案為 C，請在答案紙上塗黑作答。

31. A. 1200.
　　B. 600.
　　C. 1500.
　　D. 750.

32. A. It's Mr. King's problem.

    B. It's a family get-together.

    C. Mr. King does not know her parents.

    D. Mr. King is not sociable.

33. A. In a barbershop.

    B. In a hotel.

    C. In a foot massage salon.

    D. In a dentist clinic.

34. A. Studying in Australia.

    B. Learning surfing in Australia.

    C. Going on working holidays in Australia.

    D. Having holidays abroad.

35. A. Because of the English schools.

    B. Because of the private English teacher.

    C. Because of the English movies.

    D. Because of the English summer camp.

36. A. He has a part-time job.

    B. He got sick from his brother.

    C. His brother causes problems.

    D. He forgot his homework.

37. A. The good show on TV.

    B. The length of sleep.

    C. The time to go to bed.

    D. The quality of sleep.

38. A. When her cousin had his birthday.

    B. When her cousin came over for a visit.

    C. When her cousin went on a tour with her.

    D. When her cousin had his wedding.

39. A. It is not a good idea.

    B. It does not work for her.

    C. It is fun to go to Tokyo.

    D. It is not surprising.

40. A. Visiting their client.

    B. The woman's Chinese understanding.

    C. Their travel agency.

    D. Their travel routes.

41. A. A historical documentary.

    B. A collection of Impressionist paintings.

    C. A fantastic music concert.

    D. A palace of precious treasures.

42. A. She does not like Hualien.

 B. She does not like the company.

 C. Her family does not want to move to Hualien.

 D. Her job is tough and pays too little.

43. A. Donating old clothes to church.

 B. Buying a second-hand computer.

 C. Buying second-hand furniture to donate money.

 D. Collecting second-hand furniture for pleasure.

44. A. The man will not go mountain climbing.

 B. The woman will go mountain climbing by herself.

 C. They will help John move together.

 D. They will go mountain climbing on Sunday.

45. A. It has a nice view.

 B. It has a big sofa.

 C. It has many windows.

 D. It is clean and comfortable.

中級聽力測驗錄音稿 script-3

Track**17**

英語能力分級檢定測驗中級
聽力測驗

本測驗分三部分，全為四選一之選擇題，每部分各 15 題，共 45 題。

第一部分有 15 題，為第 1 題至第 15 題。試題冊上有數幅圖畫，每一圖畫有 1 ～ 3 個描述該圖之題目，每題請聽錄音機播出題目以及 A、B、C、D 四個英語敘述之後，選出與所看到的圖畫最相符的答案，每題只播出一遍。

例：

（看）

（聽）What is this?

　　A. This is a desk.

　　B. This is a chair.

　　C. This is a box.

　　D. This is a bed.

正確答案為 A，請在答案紙上塗黑作答。

　　A、B、C、D 四個句子中，只有句子 A 與圖片內容最相符，因此正確答案應該選 A。請在答案紙上塗黑作答。現在請翻開試題冊。

(Pause 4 seconds) 現在開始聽力測驗第一部分。

For questions number 1 and 2, please look at picture A.

Question number 1：

What does the map show?

A. The museum is next to the MRT entrance.

B. The hospital is across from the bank.

C. The MRT entrance is next to the park.

D. The movie theater is across from the bank.

Question number 2：

Look at the map again. Where is the park?

A. Go straight ahead and take the first left. You'll see it on the left.

B. Go straight ahead and take the first right. You'll see it on the right.

C. Go straight ahead and take the second left. You'll see it on the left.

D. Go straight ahead and take the second right. You'll see it on the right.

Track **18**

For question number 3 and 4, please look at picture B.

Question number 3：

Which statement about these items is correct?

A. The book costs four hundred and fifty dollars.

B. The fan costs two hundred and twenty dollars.

C. The umbrella costs five hundred and fifty dollars.

D. The cup costs one hundred and forty dollars.

Track**18**

Question number 4：

Please look at picture B again. Which comparison of these items is correct?

A. The most expensive item is the book.

B. The cup is more expensive than the book.

C. The umbrella is less expensive then the fan.

D. The book is less expensive than the umbrella.

For questions number 5, please look at picture C.

Question number 5：

Look at Mary. What is she doing?

A. She is playing with a cat.

B. She is sweeping the floor.

C. She is walking a dog.

D. She is flying a kite.

For questions number 6 and 7, please look at picture D.

Track **18**

Question number 6：

Look at John. What is he doing?

A. He's erasing the blackboard.

B. He's watching television.

C. He's cooking a meal.

D. He's typing a letter.

Question number 7：

What is the time now?

A. 6：45 p.m.

B. 7：45 p.m.

C. 8：45 p.m.

D. 9：45 p.m.

For questions number 8 and 9, please look at picture E.

Question number 8：

Look at Lucy. What is she doing?

A. She is playing the piano.

B. She is taking medicine.

C. She is reading an e-mail.

D. She is playing the flute.

第四章

聴力模擬試題

Question number 9：

What is Lucy's hairstyle?

A. She has a ponytail.

B. She has her hair in a bun.

C. She has straight hair.

D. She has short hair.

Track**19**

For questions number 10, please look at picture F.

Question number 10：

Look at the picture. What are the two women doing?

A. They are cooking together in a kitchen.

B. They are visiting a scenic spot together.

C. They are talking to each other on the phone.

D. They are sending e-mails to each other.

For questions number 11, please look at picture G.

Question number 11：

During which of the following times is the clinic closed?

A. Sunday morning.

B. Sunday afternoon.

C. Saturday afternoon.

D. Sunday evening.

Track 19

For question number 12 and 13, please look at picture H.

Question number 12：

Which statement about the woman's morning activities is correct?

A. She has breakfast before doing exercise.

B. She cleans up before doing exercise.

C. She does exercise before having breakfast.

D. She cleans up before having breakfast.

Question number 13：

Where does the woman possibly do exercise?

A. In the living room.

B. In a park.

C. In a gym.

D. In a sports center.

For questions number 14 and 15, please look at picture I.

Question number 14：

According to this pie chart, how does Jessica spend her time after school?

A. She spends most of her time playing the piano.

B. She spends more time playing the piano than doing homework.

C. She spends most of her time doing homework.

D. She spends most of her time watching television.

Question number 15：

What does she spend the same time doing as watching TV?

A. Doing homework.

B. Working out.

C. Playing the piano.

D. Having family dinner.

Track**20**

　　第二部分有 15 題，為第 16 題至第 30 題。每題請聽錄音機播出一英語問句或直述句之後，從試題冊上 A、B、C、D 四個回答或回應中，找出一個最適合的作答。每題只播出一遍。

　　請聽例題：Where is your brother now?

A. He's 20 years old.

B. He's a doctor.

C. He's thirsty.

D. He's in New York.

　　A、B、C、D 四個回答中，只有 D 是正確回答，因此正確答案應該選 D。現在開始聽力測驗第二部分。

中級 Listening Comprehension & Speaking NEW
新制全民英檢
GEPT 聽力&口說 模擬試題 +解答
The General English Proficiency Test [Intermediate]

Track**20**

16. Why did you come to school late again?

17. Where have you been recently?

18. Let's have a welcome party for Mr. Chen.

19. What are you going to wear today?

20. Where do you take your yoga lessons?

21. Have you read that English novel before?

22. Sorry, I'm late again. Can I buy you a drink?

23. When does the bank here close?

24. You've made a lot of progress in English.

25. Didn't you say you would never use Facebook?

26. What should I give her as birthday gift?

27. How many times do I have to tell you this?

28. What part-time job will you do this summer?

29. I'm going to give this book to my friend. Could you wrap it up for me?

30. Do you usually like to try new things?

第三部分有 15 題，為第 31 題至第 45 題。每題請聽錄音機播出 **Track21** 一段對話及一個相關的問題後，從試題冊上 A、B、C、D 四個備選答案中找出一個最適合的回答。每段對話及問題只播出一遍。

請聽例題：(Man)How do you go to school every day?

(Woman)Usually on foot. Sometimes by bus.

Question：How does the woman go to school?

A. She always walks to school.

B. She usually takes a bus.

C. She either walks or takes a bus.

D. She usually goes on foot,never by bus.

A、B、C、D 四個備選答案中，只有 C 是正確回答，因此正確答案應該選 C。現在開始聽力測驗第三部分。

31. W： How much does one Peking Duck cost?

    M： From Monday to Friday, 1200 Taiwan Dollars, and on the weekends, 1500 Taiwan Dollars.

    W： We'd like to order one for the dinner on the coming National Day.

    M： On public holidays,it costs the same as on the weekend.

    Q： How much does one Peking Duck cost on the National Day?

32. M： Do you want to invite Mr. King to our dinner tonight?

    W： I'd like to, but it's a family dinner, you know.

    M： Your parents have met Mr. King, haven't they?

    W： You are right, but I still don't think it's such a good idea.

    M： I guess you know your parents better than I.

    W： Maybe we can invite Mr. King over when my parents are away.

    Q： Why does the woman think it's not so good to invite Mr. King

第四章
聽力模擬試題

Track**22**

33. W： Will Oct. 16 suit you?

　　M： Not really, I'll be away from Oct. 12 to Oct. 17.

　　W： In that case, could you make it on the evening of Oct. 17?

　　M： I'll probably be too tired to do anything.

　　W： If so, for your teeth, please make sure you come here on

Oct. 18.

Q： Where does this conversation most likely take place?

34. M： I hear you are going to Australia.

　　W： That's right,but not for studies. I'll be on working holidays.

　　M： What are you going to do exactly?

　　W： The only thing I'm told is working on the farm.

Q： What are the two people talking about?

35. W： When did you start to learn English?

　　M： About the first year of elementary school, and you?

　　W： Probably the same as you.

　　M： How come you can speak English much better than us?

　　W： Maybe it's because my parents watch a lot of English movies

at home with us.

Track**22**

Q： Why does the woman think she can speak English that well?

36. W： What's wrong with you? You didn't do your homework again.

M： Sorry, I have a little brother and he gives us a hard time.

W： How old is your little brother?

W： Almost two years old.

Q： Why was the male student not able to do his homework?

37. W： What time did I ask you to go to bed?

M： Let me finish watching this show on TV, please.

W： How long will this show last?

M： About 20 more minutes.

W： Okay.

Q： What are the two people talking about?

38. M： When is last time you saw your cousin?

W： Let me see⋯The year of 2008 when my cousin had his wedding.

M： Do you think we should invite him to come here soon?

W： That's a great idea!

Q： According to the woman,when was the last time she saw her cousin?

39. M： Look at David's latest result of his English test, number one in his class!

W： Did you push him a lot?

M： Not really, but I promised him to take him to Tokyo Disneyland as a reward.

W： No wonder.

Track23

Q： What does the woman think of what the man just said?

40. M： Please don't forget we're going to visit a client together on December 10.

W： I won't. The client we are going to visit is a giant travel agency.

Track **23**

M： Thank you for coming along because I don't understand Chinese at all.

W： Don't mention it. Thanks to you,I can have this opportunity to learn.

M： You are always so kind and helpful.

Q： What are the two people talking about?

41. W： Would you like to visit the National Palace Museum with me?

M： Is there any special exhibitions at the moment?

W： Yes. Right now, a rare collection of Impressionist paintings is being shown there.

M： That sounds fantastic. Do you mind if I invite some other friends to come along?

Q： What does the woman invite the man to see in the museum?

42. M： I hear you got a job in Hualien. Congratulations! When are you going?

W： In fact,I haven't decided if I should go.

M： Why? I thought you wanted the job.

W：Yes, that job is very suitable for me, but my husband and two small kids don't want to come along.

M：I see.

Q：Why is it hard for the woman to make the decision to go to Hualien?

43. M：What are you looking on the Internet now?

W：Well, I'm looking for second-hand furniture.

M：Since when you are that interested in second-hand stuff?

W：I just think we should make good use of second-hand furniture, and donate the extra money to help the poor.

M：Awesome. I totally agree.

Track**24**

Q：What are the two people talking about?

44. W：Let's go mountain climbing.

M：My doctor told me to go to the nature, too.

W：What about this coming Saturday?

M：No, I can't. I promised John to help him move.

W：Then how about Sunday?

M： That shouldn't be any problem.

Track**24**

Q： When do the two people agree on in the end?

45. M： This is the room. You can take a close look.

W： Oh, it looks quite clean and cozy.

M： Well, you can use the bookshelf and the desk and chairs.

W： It looks really nice. May I take a look of the kitchen and bathroom?

M： Of course. You know you have to share the kitchen and bathroom with others, don't you?

W： Yes. How much is the rent?

M： It's $8,000 a month.

W： I'll take the room.

Q： Which of the following descriptions of the room is correct?

This is the end of the Listening Comprehension Test.

第三回聽力模擬試題
解答與翻譯

GEPT 中級聽力測驗（LTI-A）解答

1.D	11.D	21.D	31.C	41.B
2.C	12.C	22.D	32.B	42.C
3.C	13.B	23.C	33.D	43.C
4.D	14.C	24.D	34.C	44.D
5.D	15.C	25.D	35.C	45.D
6.B	16.A	26.D	36.C	
7.B	17.C	27.C	37.C	
8.D	18.D	28.C	38.D	
9.A	19.B	29.A	39.D	
10.C	20.A	30.C	40.A	

中級 Listening Comprehension & Speaking

NEW

新制全民英檢

GEPT

The General English Proficiency Test [Intermediate]

聽力&口說 模擬試題+解答

英語能力分級檢定測驗中級

模擬試題第三回

聽力測驗

本測驗分三部分，全為四選一之選擇題，每部分各 15 題，共 45 題。

第一部分有 15 題，為第 1 題至第 15 題。試題冊上有數幅圖畫，每一圖畫有 1 ～ 3 個描述該圖之題目，每題請聽錄音機播出題目以及 A、B、C、D 四個英語敘述之後，選出與所看到的圖畫最相符的答案，每題只播出一遍。

☆第 1 至 2 題請看 A 圖

1. 這張地圖告訴我們什麼訊息？

A. 博物館位於捷運入口的旁邊

B. 醫院位於銀行的對面

C. 捷運入口位於公園的旁邊

D. 電影院位於銀行的對面

2. 再仔細看看這張地圖，公園位於何處？

A. 直走第一個路口左轉，即可看到公園在你的左邊

B. 直走第一個路口右轉，即可看到公園在你的右邊

C. 直走第二個路口左轉，即可看到公園在你的左邊

D. 直走第二個路口右轉，即可看到公園在你的右邊

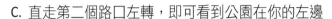第 3 至 4 題請看 B 圖

3. 下列何敘述是正確的？

A. 書的售價是 450 元

B. 扇子的售價是 220 元

C. 雨傘的售價是 550 元

D. 杯子的售價是 150 元

4. 請再看 B 圖，下列哪一個關於這些物品的比較是正確的？

A. 最貴的是書

B. 杯子比書貴

C. 雨傘比扇子便宜

D. 書比雨傘便宜

第 5 題請看 C 圖

5. 你看瑪麗在做什麼？

A. 她在和貓玩

B. 她在掃地

C. 她在遛狗

D. 她在放風箏

☆第 6 至 7 題請看 D 圖

6. 你看約翰在做什麼？

A. 他在擦黑板

B. 他在看電視

C. 他在烹飪

D. 他在寫信

7. 現在幾點？

A. 晚上六點四十五分

B. 晚上七點四十五分

C. 晚上八點四十五分

D. 晚上九點四十五分

☆第 8 至 9 題請看 E 圖

8. 你看露西在做什麼？

A. 她在彈鋼琴

B. 她在吃藥

C. 她在讀電子郵件

D. 她在吹長笛

9. 露西的髮型是怎麼樣的？

A. 她綁了個馬尾

B. 她梳了一個髮髻

C. 她留直髮

D. 她留短髮

☆第 10 題請看 F 圖

10. 你看圖中的兩個女子正在做什麼？

A. 她們正在廚房一起烹飪

B. 她們正在一起參訪觀光景點

C. 她們正在講電話

D. 她們正在傳電子郵件給對方

☆第 11 題請看 G 圖

11. 在下列哪段時間這家診所休診？

A. 星期日上午

B. 星期日下午

中級 Listening Comprehension & Speaking

新制全民英檢

GEPT

The General English Proficiency Test | Intermediate |

NEW

聽力&口說模擬試題 +解答

C. 星期六下午

D. 星期日晚上

☆第 12 至 13 題請看 H 圖

12. 下列關於這婦人晨間活動的敘述何者是正確的？

A. 她在運動前吃早餐

B. 她在運動前清掃環境

C. 她在早餐前運動

D. 她在早餐前清掃環境

13. 這婦人可能在哪裡運動？

A. 在客廳

B. 在公園

C. 在健身中心

D. 在運動中心

☆第 14 至 15 題請看 I 圖

14. 根據這張圓餅圖，潔西卡如何分配她放學後的時間？

A. 她花最多時間在彈鋼琴

B. 她花在彈鋼琴的時間比做功課多

C. 她花最多時間在做功課

D. 她花最多時間在看電視

15. 她花在什麼的時間和看電視一樣多？

A. 做功課

B. 健身

C. 彈鋼琴

D. 家庭聚餐

第二部分有 15 題，為第 16 題至第 30 題。每題請聽錄音機播出一英語問句或直述句之後，從試題冊上 A、B、C、D 四個回答或回應中，找出一個最適合的作答。每題只播出一遍。

16. 為什麼你上學又遲到了？

A. 我又睡遲了

B. 我不是做了功課了嗎？

C. 通常搭公車，有時候走路

D. 下雨天時，我搭計程車上學

17. 你最近到哪裡去了？

A. 我最近很好，你呢？

B. 最近我很懶惰

中級 Listening Comprehension & Speaking
NEW
新制全民英檢
GEPT
The General English Proficiency Test | Intermediate |
聽力&口說 模擬試題 +解答

C. 我在台灣南部待了很久

D. 你最近好嗎？

18. 我們來開個歡迎陳先生的舞會！

A. 我們會永遠記得陳先生的

B. 我會到機場為陳先生送機

C. 你會邀請陳先生嗎？

D. 好，這是個好主意

19. 妳今天要穿什麼樣的衣服？

A. 演講

B. 紫色洋裝吧

C. 在會議室

D. 會議幾點開始？

20. 你在哪裡上瑜珈課？

A. 在運動中心

B. 那套瑜珈服適合我

C. 這個決定不錯

D. 是的，瑜珈對我幫助很大

21. 那本英文小說你讀過了嗎？

A. 我想要寫一本書

B. 我到過英國兩次

C. 我不用英文寫作

D. 沒，我沒讀過那本書

22. 不好意思，我又遲到了。我可以請你喝杯飲料嗎？

A. 沒關係，你不能再來這裡

B. 我們這裡沒有那種飲料

C. 好吧，你想喝什麼樣的飲料？

D. 沒關係，下次不要遲到

23. 這裡的銀行什麼時候關門？

A. 你想要關閉你的銀行戶口嗎？

B. 靠近火車站

C. 周一至周五下午三點半

D. 周一至周五

24. 你的英文進步很多。

A. 中文比英文難多了

B. 英式下午茶是我的最愛

C. 你的英文是在哪裡學的？

D. 謝謝，我自己沒注意到

25. 你不是說你絕對不會使用臉書嗎？
A. 我從來沒聽過臉書
B. 是誰教你上網的？
C. 我沒辦法負擔臉書
D. 我不得不使用臉書，我所有的朋友都在用

26. 我應該給她什麼生日禮物呢？
A. 她會辦一個超大的慶生舞會
B. 她媽媽會給她烤個大蛋糕
C. 你可不可以跟她說我不能出席？
D. 你自己做的東西應該不錯

27. 我要重覆告訴你幾次才行？
A. 我們可以再來一次
B. 晚點我會讓你知道
C. 不好意思，我不會再犯這個錯誤
D. 你可以再告訴我一次

28. 這個夏天你會打什麼工？
A. 好，我會申請那份工作
B. 不，我不喜歡他的人格
C. 或許當女服務生

D. 我的工作讓我很忙碌

29. 我要送這本書給我的朋友，你可以幫我包裝嗎？
A. 當然可以，這張禮物包裝紙可以嗎？
B. 這不關我們的事
C. 不行，這是非賣品
D. 不行，所有的商品一旦售出不可退貨

30. 通常你喜歡嚐試新的事物嗎？
A. 對，那真是個壞消息
B. 不，我不喜歡那個新老師
C. 喜歡，我喜歡體驗新事物
D. 不，沒人喜歡那消息

　　第三部分：簡短對話，本部分共 15 題，每題請聽錄音機播出一段對話及一個相關的問題後，從試題冊上 A、B、C、D 四個備選答案中找出一個最適合的回答。每段對話及問題只播出一遍。

31.
女：一隻北京烤鴨多少錢？
男：星期一至星期五，一千兩百元台幣，周末一千五百元台幣。
女：即將來臨的國慶日晚餐，我們想要訂一隻。

男：在國訂假日和周末一樣價錢。

問題：國慶日的北京烤鴨要價多少？

A. 1200 元

B. 600 元

C. 1500 元

D. 750 元

32.

男：今晚妳想要邀請金先生來吃晚餐嗎？

女：我很想，可是你知道這是家庭聚餐。

男：妳爸媽見過金先生吧？

女：你説的對，但是我還是覺得不妥。

男：我猜妳比我還了解妳爸媽。

女：或許我們可以在我爸媽不在的時候邀請金先生。

問題：為什麼這女子認為今晚邀請金先生不妥？

A. 這是金先生的問題

B. 這是個家庭聚會

C. 金先生不認識她的父母親

D. 金先生不擅長社交

33.

女：10 月 16 日適合你嗎？

男：不太適合，10 月 12 日至 17 日我要出遠門。

女：這樣的話，你可以 10 月 17 日晚上過來嗎？

男：我可能會累到什麼也不能做。

女：那麼，為了你的牙齒，請在 10 月 18 日來這裡一趟。

問題：這段對話最可能在哪裡發生？

A. 在理髮院

B. 在飯店裡

C. 在腳底按摩院

D. 在牙醫診所

34.

男：我聽說妳要到澳洲去？

女：對，但是不是為了讀書，我是為了打工渡假去的。

男：妳到那裡究竟要做什麼？

女：我只知道是要到農場工作。

問題：這兩個人在談些什麼？

A. 在澳洲求學

B. 在澳洲學衝浪

C. 去澳洲打工渡假

D. 去國外渡假

35.

女：你是什麼時候開始學英語的？

男：大約在小學一年級時，妳呢？

女：大概和你同時候。

男：那妳的英語怎麼會比我們好那麼多呢？

女：或許是因為我爸媽和我們一起看很多英語電影吧。

問題：為什麼這個女子認為她的英語可以說得那麼好？

A. 因為英語學校

B. 因為私人英語教師

C. 因為英語電影

D. 因為英語夏令營

36.

女：你怎麼了？又沒有做功課。

男：不好意思，我有個弟弟，他把我們全家鬧得雞犬不寧。

女：你的弟弟幾歲？

男：快要滿兩歲。

問題：為什麼這個男學生沒辦法做功課？

A. 他有份兼差

B. 他被弟弟傳染生病

C. 他的弟弟造成很多問題

D. 他忘了做他的功課

37.

女：我要你什麼時候上床睡覺的？

男：請讓我看完這個電視節目。

女：這個節目還要多久結束？

男：大約二十分鐘。

女：好吧。

問題：這兩個人在討論什麼事？

A. 電視上的好節目

B. 睡眠的時間

C. 上床睡覺的時間

D. 睡眠的品質

38.

男：你上一次看到你堂哥是什麼時候？

女：讓我想想⋯2008 年我堂哥的婚禮上。

中級
新制全民英檢
GEPT
Listening Comprehension & Speaking
NEW
聽力&口說 模擬試題+解答
The General English Proficiency Test [Intermediate]

男：妳覺得我們最近該邀請他來這裡嗎？

女：真是個好主意。

問題：根據這個女子的話，上回她看到她堂哥是什麼時候？

A. 當她堂哥生日時

B. 當她堂哥過來拜訪時

C. 當她堂哥和她一起出遊時

D. 當她堂哥舉行婚禮時

39.

男：妳看大衛最近的英文考試成績，全班第一名。

女：你給了他很大的壓力嗎？

男：沒有，但是我答應帶他去東京迪斯奈樂園作為獎勵。

女：難怪。

問題：這個女子對於這男子剛才所説的話意見如何？

A. 這不是個好主意

B. 她覺得這方法對她不適用

C. 去東京很好玩

D. 怪不得

40.

男：請別忘了我們 12 月 10 日要一起去拜訪一個客戶。

女：我不會，我們要去拜訪的客戶是家規模很大的旅行社。

男：謝謝妳陪我去，因為我一點也不懂中文。

女：別這麼說，因為你的緣故我可以有這個機會學習。

男：妳總是這麼仁慈和樂於助人。

問題：這兩個人在討論什麼？

A. 拜訪他們客戶的事

B. 這個女子的中文理解力

C. 他們的旅行社

D. 他們的旅遊路線

41.

女：你想要和我一起去故宮博物院嗎？

男：現在有什麼特展嗎？

女：有的，現在有個稀有印象派系列的特展。

男：聽起來好極了。我可以帶幾個朋友一起來嗎？

問題：這個女子邀請這男子到博物館看什麼？

A. 歷史紀錄片

B. 印象派系列畫展

C. 絕佳的音樂會

D. 藏有珍貴寶藏的皇宮

42.

男：我聽說妳得到了花蓮的工作。恭喜！妳什麼時候要去那裡？

女：事實上，我還沒決定是否要去那裡。

男：為什麼呢？我以為妳想要那份工作。

女：是的，那份工作對我很合適，但是我的丈夫和兩個小小孩不想和我一起去。

男：我明白了。

問題：為什麼這個女子很難下決定去花蓮？

A. 她不喜歡花蓮

B. 她不喜歡她的公司

C. 她的家庭不想要搬去花蓮

D. 她的工作很辛苦而且薪水太低

43.

男：妳上網在搜尋什麼？

女：我正在找二手傢俱。

男：妳什麼時候開始對二手貨有興趣？

女：我只是認為我們應該好好利用二手傢俱，把多餘的錢捐給窮人。

女：很好，我完全同意。

問題：這兩個人在討論什麼？

A. 捐二手衣給教會

B. 買二手電腦

C. 買二手傢俱好捐錢

D. 因為興趣蒐集二手傢俱

44.

女：我們去爬山吧。

男：我的醫師也叫我去接近自然。

女：即將到來的這個星期六怎麼樣？

男：不行，我答應了約翰幫他搬家。

女：那麼星期日呢？

男：那應該沒問題。

問題：這兩個人最後同意怎麼做？

A. 這個男子不會去爬山

B. 這個女子要獨自去爬山

C. 他們會一起幫約翰搬家

D. 他們會在星期日去爬山

45.

男：就是這個房間，妳可以好好看清楚。

女：看起來乾淨又舒適。

男：妳可以使用這個書架和桌椅。

女：看起來真的很不錯。我可以看看廚房和廁所嗎？

男：當然，妳知道妳得要和別人共用廚房和廁所吧？

女：是的，租金多少呢？

男：一個月八千元。

女：這個房間我要了。

問題：下列關於這個房間的敘述何者為真？

A. 這個房間的風景很好

B. 這個房間有個大沙發

C. 這個房間有很多窗戶

D. 這個房間乾淨且舒適

★

CHAPTER

5

口說能力模擬試題

※ 本章共包含三回口説能力模擬試題

第一回口說能力模擬試題

英語能力分級檢定中級模擬試題
口說能力測驗

請在 15 秒內完成並唸出下列自我介紹的句子，請開始：
My registration number is (准考證號碼),and my seat number is (座位號碼).

第一部分 朗讀短文

請先利用 1 分鐘的時間閱讀下面的短文，然後在 2 分鐘內以正常的速度，清楚正確地朗讀下面的短文。

Track25

I am writing to you to thank you for the good English books published by your publishing house. About two months ago, I bought one of your English books for the first time. Since then I have recommended your English books to many classmates. Almost all my friends think highly of your books. We'd like to let you know we are all looking forward to your new English books.

***

Sport is very important. However,many people do not start to exercise until they have problems with their health. Fortunately, almost all schools have physical education in the school programs. Students can have good trainers and facilities to practice different types of sport. In this way, students do not forget to keep fit while studying.

***

In recent years, green buildings have been promoted very much because of the increasing general awareness of environmental protection.

中級
Listening Comprehension & Speaking
新制全民英檢
GEPT
The General English Proficiency Test [Intermediate]
NEW
聽力&口說 模擬試題+解答

Track25

The goal in the long run is that the sustainability of green buildings will contribute to a green city. Some experts believe that not all so-called green buildings can really conserve energy, and many owners of private buildings are therefore not sure if their "green buildings" are truly "green".

第二部分 回答問題

　　這個部分共有 10 題。題目已事先錄音，每題經由耳機播出二次，不印在試題冊上。第 1 至 5 題，每題回答時間 15 秒；第 6 至 10 題，每題回答時間 30 秒。每題播出後，請立即回答。回答時，不一定要用完整的句子，但請在作答時間內儘量表達。

第三部分 看圖敘述

下面有一張圖片及四個相關的問題，請在 1 分半鐘內完成作答。作答時，請直接回答，不需將題號及題目唸出。

1. Where are these people?

2. What are they doing?

3. Do you think they are enjoying themselves? What makes you think so?

4. If you still have time, please describe the picture in as much detail as you can.

請將下列自我介紹的句子再唸一遍，請開始：

My registration number is (准考證號碼), and my seat number is (座位號碼).

中級口說測驗錄音稿 script-1

英語能力分級檢定中級

口說能力測驗 – 1

　* 請在 15 秒內完成並唸出下列自我介紹的句子，請開始：(15" pause—beep)

第五章
口說能力模擬試題

第一部分 朗讀短文

　　請先利用 1 分鐘的時間閱讀下面的短文，然後在 2 分鐘內以正常的速度，清楚正確地朗讀下面的短文。

第二部分 回答問題

　　這個部分共有 10 題。題目已事先錄音，每題經由耳機播出二次，不印在試題冊上。第 1 至 5 題，每題回答時間 15 秒；第 6 至 10 題，每題回答時間 30 秒。每題播出後，請立即回答。回答時，不一定要用完整的句子，但請在作答時間內儘量表達。

☆第 1 至 5 題，每題回答時間 15 秒，請準備。

Question no. 1：
What did you do last weekend? (15" pause—beep)

Track**26**

Question no. 2：
What is your favorite dish? (15" pause—beep)

聽力&口說 模擬試題+解答

The General English Proficiency Test | Intermediate |

Track26

Question no. 3：

How old were you when you used knife and fork for the first time? (15" pause—beep)

Question no. 4：

In some places we should switch off our cell phones. What are some of these places? (15" pause—beep)

Track27

Question no. 5：

What would you do if someone's cell phone rings during a concert? (15" pause—beep)

☆第 6 至 10 題，每題回答時間 30 秒，請準備。

Question no. 6：

Do you prefer to study in a library or in your own room? Why? (30" pause—beep)

Question no. 7：

Why is driving under the influence of alcohol not allowed? What do you think? (30" pause—beep)

第五章

口說能力模擬試題

Question no. 8：

Do you get along with your classmates very well? What might be some good ways to make friends? (30" pause—beep)

Track**27**

Question no. 9：

Did you go to some interesting places during this summer vacation? Tell me about it. (30" pause—beep)

Question no. 10：

Would you rather read a book or watch a movie when you are free? Why? (30" pause—beep)

第二部分結束。

中級 Listening Comprehension & Speaking

NEW

新制全民英檢

GEPT

The General English Proficiency Test [Intermediate]

聽力&口說 模擬試題 +解答

第三部分 看圖敘述

下面有一張圖片及四個相關的問題，請在 1 分半鐘內完成作答。作答時，請直接回答，不需將題號及題目唸出。

首先請利用 30 秒的時間看圖及問題。(30" pause—beep)

現在請開始回答。(1'30" pause—beep)

時間到，請停止。

測驗已結束，請停止作答。請靜坐等待監考人員的指示，謝謝合作。

第一回口說能力模擬試題
解答與翻譯

GEPT 中級預試 口說能力測驗

參考答案

中級 Listening Comprehension & Speaking

NEW

新制全民英檢

GEPT

The General English Proficiency Test [Intermediate]

聽力&口說 模擬試題 +解答

第二部分 回答問題

1. I went to see a movie with my friends.

2. My favorite dish is steamed fish.

3. I began to use knife and fork when I was six.

4. We always switch off our cell phones in a library and in a concert.

5. I would ask him to switch off his cell phone.

6. I prefer to study in a library because it is very quiet there.

7. In my opinion, it is very dangerous to drive under the influence of alcohol.

8. Yes, I get along with my classmates very well. Helping people is always a good way to make friends.

9. Yes, I went to Kenting National Park with my family together, and we had a fantastic time over there.

10. I would rather watch a movie because it is more relaxing than reading a book.

第三部分 看圖敘述

They are at a traditional Taiwanese market. The man on the left seems to be a customer, and he is watching the man on the right selling his drinks. The customer looks like he is enjoying himself because he seems to be smiling. The salesman on the right is concentrating on his work. There is a basket of white sesame seeds in the front, and that shows the drinks must have white sesame seeds in them. Behind the salesman there is one advertisement notice. On the far left of the photo there is another person looking on. The salesman seems to be serving the interested passersby a sample to taste his white sesame seed drinks···

中文翻譯

英語能力分級檢定中級模擬試題
口說能力測驗

請在 15 秒內完成並唸出下列自我介紹的句子，請開始：

My registration number is（准考證號碼），and my seat number is（座位號碼）.

第五章
口說能力模擬試題

第一部分 朗讀短文

　　請先利用 1 分鐘的時間閱讀下面的短文，然後在 2 分鐘內以正常的速度，清楚正確地朗讀下面的短文。

　　我寫這封信是為了要感謝你們出版社所出版的優良英文書籍。大約兩個月前我第一次買了你們的一本英文書，從此之後，我便向很多朋友推薦。幾乎所有朋友都對你們的書評價很高，我們想要你們知道我們都很期待你們的英文新書。

　　運動是非常重要的。然而，很多人只有等到健康有問題的時候才開始運動。幸運的是，幾乎所有的學校都有體育課。學生可以有很好的教練和設備來從事不同的運動。這樣一來，學生就不會忘了讀書時要保持健康。

　　近年來人們大力提倡綠色建築，因為大眾對環境保護的意識大為提高。長久的目標是，綠建築的永續性可以對綠城市有貢獻。有些專家認為並非所有的綠建築真的可以節約能源，因此很多私人建築的所有人不甚確定他們的綠建築真的是綠色的。

中級 Listening Comprehension & Speaking

NEW

新制全民英檢

GEPT

The General English Proficiency Test | Intermediate |

聽力&口說 模擬試題+解答

第二部分 回答問題

　　這個部分共有 10 題。題目已事先錄音，每題經由耳機播出二次，不印在試題冊上。第 1 至 5 題，每題回答時間 15 秒；第 6 至 10 題，每題回答時間 30 秒。每題播出後，請立即回答。回答時，不一定要用完整的句子，但請在作答時間內儘量的表達。

☆第 1 至 5 題，每題回答時間 15 秒，請準備。

1. 你上周末做了什麼？

2. 你最喜歡的菜是哪一道？為什麼？

3. 你第一次用刀叉是幾歲的時候？

4. 在某些地方我們該關掉手機，這樣的地方有哪些？

5. 要是某人的手機在音樂會上響起來了，你會怎麼做？

☆第 6 至 10 題，每題回答時間 30 秒，請準備。

6. 你偏愛在圖書館或是在你自己的房間唸書？為什麼？

7. 為什麼酒後駕駛是不被允許的？你的意見呢？

8. 你和你的同學合得來嗎？有什麼好方法可以和人交朋友？

9. 你這個暑假到過哪些有趣的地方？告訴我你的旅遊經驗。

10. 你有空的時候比較喜歡看書還是看電影？為什麼？

答案：

1. 我和我的朋友一起去看了場電影。

2. 我最喜歡的菜是蒸魚。

3. 我六歲的時候開始學習用刀叉。

4. 在圖書館和音樂會上，我們都會關掉手機。

5. 我會要求他關掉手機。

6. 我偏愛在圖書館唸書，因為那裡很安靜。

7. 我認為酒後駕駛非常危險。

8. 是的，我和我的同學相處得很好。幫助別人總是交朋友的好方法。

9. 是的，我和我的家人一起去墾丁國家公園，我們在那邊玩得很開心。

10. 我比較喜歡看電影，因為看電影比看書輕鬆。

第五章
口說能力模擬試題

第三部分 看圖敘述

　　下面有一張圖片及四個相關的問題，請在 1 分半鐘內完成作答。作答時，請直接回答，不需將題號及題目唸出。

　　　　他們在台灣的傳統市場。左邊的男子似乎是個顧客，他正在觀看右邊的男子賣飲料。那位顧客看起來很高興，因為他的臉上似乎帶著笑容。右邊的銷售員正專心做他的工作。在前面有一籃子的亞麻籽，那表示飲料中一定含有亞麻籽。在銷售員後有張廣告宣傳單。在最左邊還有個人在觀看。銷售員似乎在倒亞麻籽茶給有興趣的路人試喝…

　　請將下列自我介紹的句子再唸一遍，請開始：

My registration number is（准考證號碼），and my seat number is（座位號碼）.

第二回口說能力模擬試題

英語能力分級檢定中級模擬試題

口說能力測驗

請在 15 秒內完成並唸出下列自我介紹的句子，請開始：

My registration number is（准考證號碼）,and my seat number is（座位號碼）.

第五章
口說能力模擬試題

第一部分 朗讀短文

Track28

請先利用 1 分鐘的時間閱讀下面的短文，然後在 2 分鐘內以正常的速度，清楚正確地朗讀下面的短文。

From this semester on, the school library will not be closed until 21：00. Students can make good use of the last thirty minutes to return and borrow books. The library used to close at 20：30, and many students complained about not having enough time to do their research in the library. Besides, library users can log on the Internet to check if they can check out the books from the library.

***

Most high schools offer cooking classes, but not many students are quite interested in learning how to cook. Most students have so much to study that they have very little time to learn new skills, such as cooking. In fact, many people do not realize the importance of cooking skills until they go abroad to study.

Track29

***

Nowadays many students have many opportunities to take part in exchange programs overseas. Quite a few high schools abroad accept exchange students from Taiwan. English-speaking countries like the United

Track29

States and Canada are the most popular choices for most Taiwanese students. Increasingly, Japan has become one of the favorite countries to choose from. No matter where you go, it is wise to learn the local language before you go.

第二部分 回答問題

　　這個部分共有 10 題。題目已事先錄音，每題經由耳機播出二次，不印在試題冊上。第 1 至 5 題，每題回答時間 15 秒；第 6 至 10 題，每題回答時間 30 秒。每題播出後，請立即回答。回答時，不一定要用完整的句子，但請在作答時間內儘量表達。

第三部分 看圖敘述

下面有一張圖片及四個相關的問題，請在 1 分半鐘內完成作答。
作答時，請直接回答，不需將題號及題目唸出。

1. Where is the man?

2. What is the man doing?

3. Do you think he looks relaxed? What makes you think so?

4. If you still have time, please describe the picture in as much detail
as you can.

請將下列自我介紹的句子再唸一遍，請開始：

My registration number is（准考證號碼）, and my seat number is（座
位號碼）.

中級 Listening Comprehension & Speaking
NEW
新制全民英檢
GEPT
The General English Proficiency Test [Intermediate]
聽力&口說 模擬試題 +解答

中級口說測驗錄音稿 script-2

英語能力分級檢定中級

口說能力測驗－2

＊請在 15 秒內完成並唸出下列自我介紹的句子，請開始：(15"
pause—beep)

第五章
口說能力模擬試題

第一部分 朗讀短文

請先利用 1 分鐘的時間閱讀下面的短文,然後在 2 分鐘內以正常的速度,清楚正確地朗讀下面的短文。

第二部分 回答問題

這個部分共有 10 題。題目已事先錄音,每題經由耳機播出二次,不印在試題冊上。第 1 至 5 題,每題回答時間 15 秒;第 6 至 10 題,每題回答時間 30 秒。每題播出後,請立即回答。回答時,不一定要用完整的句子,但請在作答時間內儘量表達。

☆第 1 至 5 題,每題回答時間 15 秒,請準備。

Question no. 1:
Where did you go last Sunday morning? (15" pause—beep)

Track**30**

Question no. 2:
Do you play any music instrument? (15" pause—beep)

Track**30**

Question no. 3：

How often do you go hiking? (15" pause—beep)

Question no. 4：

Do you like to learn handicrafts? Why? (15" pause—beep)

Question no. 5：

What would you do if someone next to you hurt his own finger? (15" pause—beep)

☆第 6 至 10 題，每題回答時間 30 秒，請準備。

Question no. 6：

When and where did you start to learn English for the first time? Did you like it? (30" pause—beep)

Question no. 7：

Why is smoking not good for health? What do you think? (30" pause—beep)

Question no. 8：

Do you usually do very well in class? Do you sometimes help the classmates, who do not do as well as you? (30" pause—beep)

Question no. 9：

What hobbies do you have? Are they mostly indoor or outdoor activities? (30" pause—beep)

Track**30**

Question no. 10：

Where in Taiwan would you take your foreign visitors to if you have the chance? Why? (30" pause—beep)

第二部分結束。

第三部分 看圖敘述

下面有一張圖片及四個相關的問題,請在 1 分半鐘內完成作答。作答時,請直接回答,不需將題號及題目唸出。

首先請利用 30 秒的時間看圖及問題。(30" pause—beep)

現在請開始回答。(1'30" pause—beep)

時間到,請停止。

測驗已結束,請停止作答。請靜坐等待監考人員的指示,謝謝合作。

第二回口說能力模擬試題
解答與翻譯

GEPT 中級預試 口說能力測驗

參考答案

中級 Listening Comprehension & Speaking

NEW

新制全民英檢

GEPT

The General English Proficiency Test [Intermediate]

聽力&口說 模擬試題 +解答

第二部分 回答問題

1. I went hiking with my friends last Sunday morning.

2. Yes, I play the piano very well.

3. I go hiking about twice in a month.

4. Yes, I like to learn handicraft because it is fun.

5. I would look for a first aid kit for him.

6. I began to learn English at 8 years old, and I enjoyed it very much.

7. Smoking can cause many illnesses and is really bad for health.

8. Yes, I usually get high grades, and I often help my classmates with their homework.

9. I have many hobbies, and most of them are outdoor activities, such as cycling.

10. I would take them to the Sun Yat-sen Memorial Hall because it is a nice tourist spot.

第三部分 看圖敘述

The man is standing at the entrance of one Taipei MRT station. He is holding an EasyCard in order to enter the gateway to take the MRT train. He looks relaxed from his facial expression and his casual way of dressing. It is not very crowded inside the MRT station. It looks very clean and comfortable there. On the right side of the station inside there is a public toilet…

中文翻譯

英語能力分級檢定中級模擬試題
口說能力測驗

請在 15 秒內完成並唸出下列自我介紹的句子，請開始：

My registration number is（准考證號碼），and my seat number is（座位號碼）.

第五章
口說能力模擬試題

第一部分 朗讀短文

　　請先利用 1 分鐘的時間閱讀下面的短文，然後在 2 分鐘內以正常的速度，清楚正確地朗讀下面的短文。

　　從這學期開始，學校的圖書館將開到晚上九點。學生可以用最後的三十分鐘來借還書。以往圖書館到晚上八點半關門，很多學生抱怨沒有足夠時間在圖書館做研究。除此之外，使用圖書館的人可以從網際網路上查看他們是否能從圖書館借書。

　　大部分高中提供烹飪課，但是很多學生對學習烹飪不是很有興趣。大部分學生要唸的書太多，以至於他們沒有什麼時間學新的技能，例如烹飪。事實上，很多人直到出國唸書才明白烹飪的重要。

　　現在的學生有很多參加國際交換學生計劃的機會，有不少國外的學校接受台灣的交換學生。像是美國和加拿大的英語系國家是最受台灣學生歡迎的選擇。日本漸漸成為學生喜歡選擇的國家。無論你要到哪裡，先學習當地語言是明智之舉。

第二部分 回答問題

　　這個部分共有 10 題。題目已事先錄音，每題經由耳機播出二次，不印在試題冊上。第 1 至 5 題，每題回答時間 15 秒；第 6 至 10 題，每題回答時間 30 秒。每題播出後，請立即回答。回答時，不一定要用完整的句子，但請在作答時間內儘量表達。

☆第 1 至 5 題，每題回答時間 15 秒，請準備。

1. 你上周日早上去了哪裡？

2. 你會彈奏什麼樂器？

3. 你多久去健行一次？

4. 你喜歡學手工藝嗎？為什麼？

5. 如果你旁邊的人手指受傷了，你會怎麼做？

☆第 6 至 10 題，每題回答時間 30 秒，請準備。

6. 你第一次學英語是在什麼時候和什麼地方？

那時候你喜歡英語嗎？

7. 為什麼抽菸對健康不好？你認為呢？

8. 你在班上表現好嗎？你有時候會幫助班上比你差的同學嗎？

9. 你有什麼興趣？你的興趣大部分是戶內還是戶外的活動？

10. 如果你有機會帶外國訪客參觀台灣，你會帶他們到哪裡？
為什麼？

答案：

1. 上星期天早上我和我朋友去健行。

2. 是的，我鋼琴彈得很好。

3. 我大概一個月去健行兩次。

4. 喜歡，我喜歡學手工藝，因為手工藝很好玩。

5. 我會為他找急救箱。

6. 我八歲的時候開始學英語，我非常喜歡英語。

7. 抽菸會造成很多疾病，對健康真的很不好。

8. 是的，我常得到高分，而且我經常幫助我的同學做功課。

9. 我有很多興趣，大部分是戶外活動，像是騎單車。

10. 我會帶他們去國父紀念館，因為那是個很好的觀光景點。

第五章
口說能力模擬試題

第三部分 看圖敘述

下面有一張圖片及四個相關的問題，請在 1 分半鐘內完成作答。作答時，請直接回答，不需將題號及題目唸出。

這個男子正站在某個台北捷運車站入口處。他正拿著一張悠遊卡要進閘門好搭捷運。從他的面部表情和他的休閒裝扮看來，他很悠閒。捷運車站內部不會很擁擠，看起來很乾淨而且很舒適。捷運車站內部右邊有個公共廁所…

請將下列自我介紹的句子再唸一遍，請開始：

My registration number is（准考證號碼）, and my seat number is（座位號碼）.

中級 Listening Comprehension & Speaking
NEW
新制全民英檢
GEPT
The General English Proficiency Test [Intermediate]
聽力&口說 模擬試題+解答

第三回口說能力模擬試題

英語能力分級檢定中級模擬試題

口說能力測驗

請在 15 秒內完成並唸出下列自我介紹的句子，請開始：

My registration number is（准考證號碼）,and my seat number is（座位號碼）.

第一部分 朗讀短文

請先利用 1 分鐘的時間閱讀下面的短文，然後在 2 分鐘內以正常 Track**31**
的速度，清楚正確地朗讀下面的短文。

Many high school students do not know what to major in in colleges. They should think carefully about what they like and don't like to study before making the decision. Student counseling can often help students understand themselves. College fairs also provide students with what students need to know about all sorts of departments in colleges.

***

Whatever one majors in, English is an important tool. English is an international language, and it opens up many possibilities. Almost all types of work require basic level of English communication skills. These days with Track**32** the Internet and many technological supports, there is no excuse for not learning English well.

***

More and more students take part in English tests in order to see

Track**32**

their English levels. In the process of preparing for the tests, it is important to make good use of the contents of the learning materials. Try to practice in daily life what you learn from the books. By doing so, your test results can really reflect what you know about English.

第二部分 回答問題

　　這個部分共有 10 題。題目已事先錄音，每題經由耳機播出二次，不印在試題冊上。第 1 至 5 題，每題回答時間 15 秒；第 6 至 10 題，每題回答時間 30 秒。每題播出後，請立即回答。回答時，不一定要用完整的句子，但請在作答時間內儘量表達。

第五章
口說能力模擬試題

第三部分 看圖敘述

下面有一張圖片及四個相關的問題，請在 1 分半鐘內完成作答。作答時，請直接回答，不需將題號及題目唸出。

1. Where are these people?

2. What are they doing?

3. Do you think they are enjoying themselves? What makes you think so?

4. If you still have time, please describe the picture in as much detail as you can.

請將下列自我介紹的句子再唸一遍，請開始：

My registration number is (准考證號碼) , and my seat number is（座位號碼）

中級口説測驗錄音稿 script-3

英語能力分級檢定中級

口説能力測驗－3

* 請在 15 秒內完成並唸出下列自我介紹的句子，請開始：(15"
pause—beep)

第五章

口說能力模擬試題

第一部分 朗讀短文

請先利用 1 分鐘的時間閱讀下面的短文，然後在 2 分鐘內以正常的速度，清楚正確地朗讀下面的短文。

第二部分 回答問題

這個部分共有 10 題。題目已事先錄音，每題經由耳機播出二次，不印在試題冊上。第 1 至 5 題，每題回答時間 15 秒；第 6 至 10 題，每題回答時間 30 秒。每題播出後，請立即回答。回答時，不一定要用完整的句子，但請在作答時間內儘量表達。

☆第 1 至 5 題，每題回答時間 15 秒，請準備。

Question no. 1：
What are you going to do this weekend? (15" pause—beep)

Track**33**

Question no. 2：
Do you know how to bake? (15" pause—beep)

Track**33**

Question no. 3：

Have you learned a second foreign language? If so,what language is it? (15" pause—beep)

Question no. 4：

Do you like camping? Why? (15" pause—beep)

Question no. 5：

What would you do if your house caught on fire? (15" pause—beep)

☆第 6 至 10 題，每題回答時間 30 秒，請準備。

Question no. 6：

What kinds of books do you like to read? Why? (30" pause—beep)

Question no. 7：

Why is it important to learn swimming? What do you think? (30" pause—beep)

Question no. 8：

Do you usually stay calm or do you get nervous easily? What do you do to not get nervous? (30" pause—beep)

Question no. 9：

Which subject is your favorite subject in school? Why? (30" pause—beep)

Question no. 10：

Where do you usually meet up with your friends? Why? (30" pause—beep)

第二部分結束。

中級
Listening
Comprehension
& Speaking
NEW
新制全民英檢
GEPT
The General English Proficiency Test | Intermediate |
聽力&口說 模擬試題 +解答

第三部分 看圖敘述

下面有一張圖片及四個相關的問題，請在 1 分半鐘內完成作答。作答時，請直接回答，不需將題號及題目唸出。

首先請利用 30 秒的時間看圖及問題。(30" pause—beep)

現在請開始回答。(1'30" pause—beep)

時間到，請停止。

測驗已結束，請停止作答。請靜坐等待監考人員的指示，謝謝合作。

第三回口說能力模擬試題
解答與翻譯

GEPT 中級預試 口說能力測驗

參考答案

第二部分 回答問題

1. I'm going to visit my aunt this weekend.

2. No, I don't know how to bake,but I'd like to learn.

3. Yes, I have learned a little bit Japanese.

4. Yes, I like camping very much because it is so much fun.

5. I would call 119 if my house caught on fire.

6. I enjoy reading science fictions because they help me learn many new things.

7. It is very important to learn swimming so that you can protect yourself.

8. Usually I can stay calm. If I get nervous, I breathe deeply to calm down.

9. My favorite subject is English because I like to learn a different

culture.

10. I usually meet up with my friends in a fast food restaurant because they are clean and not too expensive.

第三部分 看圖敘述

They are on the track of a mountain and are riding bicycles together. Their outfits look very professional. It seems that they are enjoying themselves cycling slowly in the green scenery. The weather is very nice and is great for riding bikes outdoors. They are riding upwards in a group…

中級 Listening Comprehension & Speaking

新制全民英檢

GEPT

The General English Proficiency Test [Intermediate]

NEW

聽力&口說 模擬試題 +解答

中文翻譯

英語能力分級檢定中級模擬試題
口說能力測驗

請在 15 秒內完成並唸出下列自我介紹的句子，請開始：

My registration number is（准考證號碼）, and my seat number is（座位號碼）.

第五章
口說能力模擬試題

第一部分 朗讀短文

請先利用 1 分鐘的時間閱讀下面的短文，然後在 2 分鐘內以正常的速度，清楚正確的朗讀下面的短文。

很多高中生不知道上大學要主修什麼。他們應該要在決定前好好想想他們想要和不想要學習的科目。學生諮商經常可以幫助學生更加了解自己。大學博覽會也提供了學生大學不同科系的資訊。

無論主修什麼，英語都是一個重要的工具。英語是一個國際語言，開啟了很多的機會。幾乎所有的工作都需要基本的英語溝通能力。現在有網際網路和很多支援的科技，沒有不能學好英語的藉口。

越來越多學生參加英語考試來檢定他們的英語程度。在準備考試的過程中，很重要的是要好好活用學習資料的內容。試著在日常生活中練習你在書中學到的東西。這樣的話，你的英文成績就能真正反應出你的英語程度。

中級 Listening Comprehension & Speaking
新制全民英檢
GEPT
The General English Proficiency Test [Intermediate]

NEW

聽力&口說 模擬試題 +解答

第二部分 回答問題

這個部分共有 10 題。題目已事先錄音，每題經由耳機播出二次，不印在試題冊上。第 1 至 5 題，每題回答時間 15 秒；第 6 至 10 題，每題回答時間 30 秒。每題播出後，請立即回答。回答時，不一定要用完整的句子，但請在作答時間內儘量的表達。

☆第 1 至 5 題，每題回答時間 15 秒，請準備。

1. 你這個周末要做什麼？

2. 你知道如何烘焙嗎？

3. 你學過第二外語嗎？如果有，是什麼語言？

4. 你喜歡露營嗎？為什麼？

5. 如果你的房子著火了，你會怎麼做？

☆第 6 至 10 題，每題回答時間 30 秒，請準備。

6. 你喜歡讀哪些書？為什麼？

7. 為什麼學游泳很重要？你認為呢？

8. 你通常很冷靜或很容易緊張？你會做什麼來避免緊張？

9. 你在學校最喜歡的科目是什麼？為什麼？

10. 你通常和你的朋友在哪裡碰面？為什麼？

答案：

1. 這個周末我要去拜訪我的姑姑。

2. 不，我不知道如何烘焙，但是我想學。

3. 學過，我學過一點日文。

4. 喜歡，我很喜歡露營，因為露營很好玩。

5. 如果我的房子著火了，我會打 119。

6. 我喜歡讀科幻小說，因為我可以學到很多新事物。

中級 Listening Comprehension & Speaking
NEW
新制全民英檢
GEPT
The General English Proficiency Test | Intermediate |
聽力&口說 模擬試題 +解答

7. 學游泳很重要，這樣你才能保護自己。

8. 通常我能夠保持冷靜。如果我緊張起來，我會深呼吸冷靜下來。

9. 我最喜歡的科目是英文，因為我喜歡學習新的文化。

10. 我通常和我的朋友在速食店碰面，因為速食店乾淨而且不會太貴。

第三部分 看圖敘述

下面有一張圖片及四個相關的問題，請在 1 分半鐘內完成作答。作答時，請直接回答，不需將題號及題目唸出。

他們在山間道路上，正在一起騎單車。他們的配備看起來很專業。他們似乎很享受在綠野中慢騎。天氣很好，非常適合在戶外騎單車。他們一群人正在騎上坡…

請將下列自我介紹的句子再唸一遍，請開始：

My registration number is（准考證號碼）, and my seat number is（座位號碼）.

中級
Listening
Comprehension
& Speaking

NEW

新制全民英檢
GEPT

The General English Proficiency Test [Intermediate]

聽力&口說 模擬試題+解答

CHAPTER

★

6

520 個最常考的
中級字彙

中級 Listening Comprehension & Speaking

NEW

新制全民英檢

GEPT
The General English Proficiency Test [Intermediate]

聽力&口說 模擬試題 +解答

Track**34**

A

absence n. 缺席，缺乏

【同義詞】

nonattendance, nonresidence, nonappearance, unavailability

absolute a. 純粹的；完全的

【同義詞】

complete, perfect, thorough, total

absorb v. 吸收

【同義詞】

incorporate, sponge, assimilate

abuse v. 虐待；濫用

【同義詞】

injure, damage, mistreat, maltreat

academic a. 大學的；學術的

【同義詞】

educational, learned, scholarly

acceptable a. 可以接受的；值得接受的

【同義詞】

worthy, deserving, competent

access n. 接近，進入；接近的機會或權利

【同義詞】

admission, entrance, entry

accommodation n. 住處；適應

【同義詞】

housing, lodging, residence; adaptation, adjustmet, compromise

accompany v. 陪同，伴隨

【同義詞】

escort, join, come along

accomplish v. 完成，實現，達到

【同義詞】

realize, do, complete, perform

accountant n. 會計師；會計人員

【同義詞】

bookkeeper, auditor, controller

accuracy n. 正確（性）；準確（性）

【同義詞】

accurateness, exactness, exactitude, precision

ache v. 疼痛

【同義詞】

hurt, suffer

achievement n. 達成；完成

【同義詞】

accomplishment, feat, deed, act

Track**35**

acquaintance   n.   相識的人，熟人

【同義詞】

colleague, associate, peer, teammate

adapt   v.   使適應，使適合

【同義詞】

modify, adjust, alter, vary

additional   a.   添加的；附加的；額外的

【同義詞】

supplementary, supplemental, extra

adequate   a.   足夠的

【同義詞】

satisfactory, sufficient, enough, plenty

adjust   v.   調節；改變... 以適應

【同義詞】

alter, vary, arrange, change

administration   n.   管理，經營；監督

【同義詞】

direction, management, organization, supervision

admiration   n.   欽佩，讚美，羨慕

【同義詞】

appreciation, approval, compliment, esteem, praise, respect

admission   n.   進入許可

Track**35**

【同義詞】

fee, cost, charge, bill

advanced　　a.　在前面的；高級的

【同義詞】

forward, improved, bettered, developed

adventure　　n.　冒險，冒險精神

【同義詞】

venture, take chances

advertise　　v.　廣告；宣傳

【同義詞】

announce, notify, promote, publicize

adviser　　n.　顧問；勸告者

【同義詞】

counsellor, guidance counsellor, mentor, confidant

affect　　v.　影響；對 . . . 發生作用

【同義詞】

influence, sway, move, touch

afford　　v.　買得起；有足夠的 . . .

【同義詞】

have the means, offer, furnish, supply

afterward　　adv.　之後，以後，後來

【同義詞】

中級 Listening Comprehension & Speaking
新制全民英檢 NEW
GEPT 聽力&口說 模擬試題 +解答
The General English Proficiency Test | Intermediate |

Track**36**

subsequently, after, then, next

agency　　n.　代辦處，經銷處，代理機構

【同義詞】

operation, office, work, management

aggressive　　a.　侵略的，侵犯的

【同義詞】

combative, offensive, hostile

agreement　　n.　同意，一致

【同義詞】

bargain, contract, pact, alliance

alcohol　　n.　酒精

【同義詞】

liquor, spirits

alley　　n.　小巷，胡同；後街

【同義詞】

passageway, opening

allowance　　n.　津貼，補貼；零用錢

【同義詞】

allotment, portion, grant, fee

altitude　　n.　高度；高處，高地

【同義詞】

height

ambassador　　n.　大使；使節

【同義詞】

diplomat, attache, envoy

Track**36**

ambition　　n.　雄心，抱負

【同義詞】

aspiration, hoping, wishfulness, desire

amusement　　n.　樂趣；興味

【同義詞】

entertainment, delight, pleasure, fun

analysis　　n.　分析；分解；解析

【同義詞】

examination, investigation, review

ancestor　　n.　祖宗，祖先

【同義詞】

forefather, forbear

angle　　n.　角；角度

【同義詞】

perspective, position, standpoint, viewpoint

anniversary　　n.　週年紀念；週年紀念日

【同義詞】

birthday, centenary

announce　　v.　宣佈，發佈

中級
Listening Comprehension & Speaking
新制全民英檢
NEW
GEPT
聽力&口說 模擬試題+解答
The General English Proficiency Test | Intermediate |

Track**37**

【同義詞】

proclaim, broadcast, report, state

annoy   v.   惹惱，使生氣

【同義詞】

tease, disturb, irritate

annual   a.   一年的；一年一次的

【同義詞】

yearly, anniversary

anxiety   n.   焦慮，掛念

【同義詞】

uneasiness

apology   n.   道歉；陪罪

【同義詞】

excuse, justification

apparent   a.   表面的，外觀的；未必真實的

【同義詞】

plain, clear, seeming, obvious

appeal   v.   呼籲，懇求

【同義詞】

entreat, implore, plead, beg

appetite   n.   食慾，胃口

【同義詞】

hunger, desire, craving

application　　　n.　應用，適用；運用

【同義詞】

Track**37**

use, utilization, employment, attention

appointment　　　n.　約會

【同義詞】

date, get-together, meeting

appreciation　　　n.　欣賞，鑑賞；賞識

【同義詞】

esteem, respect, taste, understanding

approach　　　n.　接近，靠近

【同義詞】

advance, entrance

appropriate　　　a.　適當的，恰當的，相稱的

【同義詞】

suitable, becoming, fitting, proper

approve　　　v.　贊成，同意；贊許

【同義詞】

endorse, ratify, sanction, accredit

architecture　　　n.　建築學；建築術

【同義詞】

structure, construction, building

中級 Listening Comprehension & Speaking
NEW
新制全民英檢
GEPT
The General English Proficiency Test [Intermediate]

聽力&口說 模擬試題 +解答

Track**38**

argument   n.   爭吵；辯論

【同義詞】

debate, disagreement, dispute

arrangement   n.   安排；準備工作

【同義詞】

order, organization, system, classification

arrow   n.   箭

【同義詞】

shaft, bolt

artificial   a.   人工的，人造的；假的

【同義詞】

false, pretended, unreal, substitute

artistic   a.   藝術的；美術的；唯美（主義）的

【同義詞】

attractive, lovely, handsome, masterly

assignment   n.   （分派的）任務；工作

【同義詞】

duty, responsibility, task

assistance   n.   援助，幫助

【同義詞】

help, aid, avail, service

association   n.   協會，公會，社團

【同義詞】

alliance, body, club, company

athlete   n.   運動員，體育家

Track**38**

【同義詞】

sportsman, player

atmosphere   n.   氣氛

【同義詞】

environment, feeling, mood, vibes

attachment   n.   連接；安裝；附件

【同義詞】

accessory, addition, supplement

attempt   v.   試圖；企圖；試圖做

【同義詞】

try, endeavor, undertake, strive

attitude   n.   態度，意見，看法

【同義詞】

viewpoint, standpoint, position, opinion

attract   v.   吸引

【同義詞】

tempt, charm, allure, fascinate

author   n.   作者；作家

【同義詞】

中級 Listening Comprehension & Speaking NEW
新制全民英檢
GEPT 聽力&口說 模擬試題+解答
The General English Proficiency Test [Intermediate]

Track**39**

writer, composer, scribbler, penman

average　　n.　一般，普通；中等

【同義詞】

usual, common, ordinary, general

awake　　v.　清醒的；意識到的

【同義詞】

active, conscious, alert, wakeful

award　　n.　獎，獎品；獎狀

【同義詞】

reward, prize, medal, trophy

awful　　a.　可怕的，嚇人的

【同義詞】

brutal, ruthless, terrible, horrible

awkward　　a.　笨拙的；不熟練的，不靈巧的

【同義詞】

clumsy, cumbersome, ungraceful

B

babysit　　n.　當臨時保姆

【同義詞】

care for a child

background   n.   背景；出身背景，學經歷

【同義詞】

practice, knowledge, training, experience

Track**39**

backup   n.   備用，備用物；後援，支持

【同義詞】

fill-in, relief, reserve, stand-in, substitute

backward   a. adv.   向後的，反向的，返回的

【同義詞】

rearward, in reverse, retrogressively, reversed

baggage   n.   行李

【同義詞】

luggage, packages, pack, bags

balance   n.   平衡，均衡

【同義詞】

harmony, level, match

balcony   n.   陽臺，露臺

【同義詞】

porch, veranda, terrace, deck

bald   a.   禿頭的，禿頂的

【同義詞】

open, uncovered, hairless, simple

balloon   v.   像氣球般鼓起（或膨脹）

【同義詞】

inflate, swell, swell out

Track**40**

ban   v.   禁止；禁令

【同義詞】

bar, disallow, forbid, inhibit, outlaw, prohibit

bandage   v.   用繃帶包紮

【同義詞】

dress, compress

bankrupt   a.   破產的；有關破產的

【同義詞】

broke, destitute, impoverished, insolvent, poor

bare   a.   裸的

【同義詞】

naked, open, nude, bald

bargain   n.   協議；買賣，交易；便宜貨

【同義詞】

agreement, barter, deal, sale, transaction

bathe   v.   把...浸入，浸洗

【同義詞】

swim, launder, rinse, cover

bat   v.   用球棒或球拍打球

【同義詞】

knock, strike, hit

battle n. 戰鬥；戰役

【同義詞】

contest, conflict, struggle, fight

Track**40**

bay n. （海或湖泊的）灣

【同義詞】

harbour, cove, gulf

beast n. 獸，野獸

【同義詞】

animal, creature

beauty n. 美，美麗，優美

【同義詞】

loveliness, comeliness, fairness, prettiness

beg v. 乞討

【同義詞】

appeal, beseech, plead, implore

behavior n. 行為，舉止；態度

【同義詞】

conduct, action, deportment, acts

belly n. 腹部；肚子

【同義詞】

abdomen, stomach, paunch

Track**40**

bend　　v.　使彎曲，折彎

【同義詞】

curve, turn, bow, stoop

beneath　　prep.　... 之下；（地位等）低於，劣於

【同義詞】

below, under

biscuit　　n.　小麵包；軟餅

【同義詞】

cookie, cooky

bleed　　v.　出血，流血

【同義詞】

drain, exhaust, grieve, pity

bless　　v.　為 ... 祝福，為 ... 祈神賜福

【同義詞】

praise, glorify, thank

blossom　　v.　開花

【同義詞】

develop, flower, bloom

blush　　v.　臉紅

【同義詞】

redden, colour, flush, crimson

boast　　v.　自吹自擂；誇耀

【同義詞】

brag, show off

bold　　a.　英勇的，無畏的；大膽的　　Track**41**

【同義詞】

defiant, impudent, brazen, arrogant

bookshelf　　n.　書架；書櫃

【同義詞】

bookcase

bookstore　　n.　書店

【同義詞】

bookshop, bookstall

bow　　v.　鞠躬，欠身

【同義詞】

stoop, bend, kneel

brand　　n.　商標；牌子

【同義詞】

mark, label, burn, tag

bravery　　n.　勇敢，勇氣

【同義詞】

courage, gallantry, boldness, daring

breast　　n.　乳房

【同義詞】

Track**41**

chest, bosom, front

breathe　　　v.　呼吸；呼氣；吸氣

【同義詞】

respire, puff, pant, wheeze

briefcase　　n.　公事包

【同義詞】

attache case

brilliant　　　a.　光輝的，明亮的；傑出的，出色的

【同義詞】

sparkling, bright, shining, clear

bubble　　n.　水泡，氣泡，泡

【同義詞】

glob, drop, droplet

budget　　n.　預算；預算費；生活費，經費

【同義詞】

ration, allowance, schedule

bulletin　　n.　公報；公告

【同義詞】

message, circular, news, statement

bump　　v.　碰，撞

【同義詞】

hit, shake, push, collide

bunch　　n.　串，束

【同義詞】

cluster, group, set, batch

Track**42**

burger　　n.　漢堡

【同義詞】

hamburger

C

cabin　　n.　客艙

【同義詞】

hut, cottage, bungalow, house

calculate　　v.　計算

【同義詞】

count, figure, compute, estimate

camping　　n.　去露營

【同義詞】

tenting

candidate　　n.　候選人；候補者

【同義詞】

seeker, nominee, applicant

capable　　a.　有 ... 的能力

Track42

【同義詞】

intelligent, apt, smart, clever

cape   a.   披肩；斗篷

【同義詞】

cloak, mantle

cashier   n.   出納，出納員

【同義詞】

teller, banker, cambist, treasurer

casual   a.   偶然的，碰巧的

【同義詞】

accidental, chance, unexpected

catalog   n.   目錄；目錄冊，目錄簿

【同義詞】

list, classify, record, group

cattle   n.   牛

【同義詞】

livestock, stock, cows

cave   n.   洞穴，洞窟

【同義詞】

lair, shelter, den, cavern

celebration   n.   慶祝

【同義詞】

feast, festivity, party

certificate n. 證明書；執照；結業證書

【同義詞】

document, testimonial, certification, documentation

Track**43**

chain n. 鏈，鏈條；項圈

【同義詞】

band, bind, bond

challenge n. 挑戰

【同義詞】

competition, contest

champion n. 優勝者，冠軍

【同義詞】

winner, victor, choice, best

charity n. 慈悲，仁愛，博愛；慈善

【同義詞】

generosity, liberality, liberalness

charm n. 魅力

【同義詞】

attractiveness, appeal, allure, allurement

chat v. 閒談，聊天

【同義詞】

gossip, talk, converse

中級 Listening Comprehension & Speaking

NEW

新制全民英檢

GEPT

The General English Proficiency Test [Intermediate]

聽力&口說 模擬試題+解答

Track**43**

| check | n. | 檢查，檢驗，核對 |

【同義詞】

stop, control, restrain, curb

| cheek | n. | 臉頰；腮幫子 |

【同義詞】

jaw

| cheerful | a. | 興高采烈的；情緒好的 |

【同義詞】

cheery, gay, sunny

| chemist | n. | 化學家；藥劑師，藥商 |

【同義詞】

druggist, pharmacist

| cherish | v. | 珍愛；撫育；愛護 |

【同義詞】

adore, worship, treasure, protect

| chess | n. | 西洋棋 |

【同義詞】

chess game

| chest | n. | 胸，胸膛；箱子，盒子 |

【同義詞】

box, locker, dresser, safe

| chew | v. | 嚼，咀嚼，嚼碎 |

【同義詞】

bite, grind, munch, nibble

chore   n. 家庭雜務；農莊雜務

Track**44**

【同義詞】

task, job, work, duty

chorus   n. 合唱隊

【同義詞】

choir, group, unison

cigarette   n. 香煙，紙煙，煙卷

【同義詞】

smoke, butt, cig, weed

cinema   n. 電影院

【同義詞】

motion picture, cine, film, movie

circular   a. 圓的，圓形的；環形的

【同義詞】

round, annular, ring-shaped

circus   n. 馬戲團；馬戲表演

【同義詞】

big top, carnival, rodeo, troupe

clinic   n. 診所，門診所

【同義詞】

Track**44**

infirmary, hospital, medical center

clown   n.   小丑，丑角

【同義詞】

fool, play, comic, performer

clue   n.   線索，跡象，提示

【同義詞】

hint, evidence, proof, sign

clumsy   a.   笨拙的，手腳不靈活的

【同義詞】

awkward, ungraceful, ungainly, cumbersome

code   n.   法典，法規；代碼，密碼

【同義詞】

laws, rules, system, signal

coincidence   n.   巧合；巧事；同時發生

【同義詞】

correspondence, identity, similarity

collar   n.   衣領

【同義詞】

neckband

colleague   n.   聯合；加盟

【同義詞】

co-worker, collaborator, fellow-worker

comfort   v.   安慰，慰問

【同義詞】

console, ease, assure, relieve

Track**45**

commerce   n.   商業，貿易，交易

【同義詞】

trade, business, dealings

communication   n.   傳達；通信；傳染

【同義詞】

message, notice, report, statement

companion   n.   同伴，伴侶；朋友

【同義詞】

partner, accompanist, buddy, friend

comparison   n.   比較，對照；類似

【同義詞】

contrast, collation, confronting, likening

competition   n.   競爭，角逐

【同義詞】

contest, game, match, tournament

comprehension   n.   理解；理解力

【同義詞】

understanding, apprehension, intelligence, grasp

concentration   n.   集中

Track45

【同義詞】

clustering, collection, massing

concept　　n.　概念，觀念，思想

【同義詞】

thought, notion, idea, opinion

concert　　n.　音樂會，演奏會

【同義詞】

music, recital

condition　　n.　情況；（健康等）狀態

【同義詞】

provision, specification, state, circumstance

conduct　　v.　引導，帶領

【同義詞】

manage, direct, guide, lead

conference　　n.　會議；討論會，協商會

【同義詞】

meeting, convention, council, caucus

confidence　　n.　自信，信心，把握

【同義詞】

trust, faith, reliance, dependence

congratulate　　v.　祝賀；恭禧

【同義詞】

第六章

520 個最常考的

bless, compliment, flatter, commend

connect v. 連接，連結

【同義詞】

Track**45**

join, unite, combine, link

consideration n. 考慮

【同義詞】

attention, notice, advertency, examination

consult v. 與...商量

【同義詞】

confer, discuss, talk over

consumer n. 消費者；消耗者

【同義詞】

user, buyer, purchaser, shopper

coward n. 懦夫，膽怯者

【同義詞】

weakling

crash v. 碰撞，倒下，墜落

【同義詞】

strike, shatter, break, smash

credit n. 信譽；信用，榮譽；功勞

【同義詞】

belief, trust, faith, honor

Track**46**

creep　　v.　躡手躡足地走；緩慢地行進

【同義詞】

crawl

criticize　　v.　批評；批判；苛求；非難

【同義詞】

judge, appraise, assess

crown　　n.　王冠；王位

【同義詞】

cap, peak, summit, tip, top

cue　　n.　提示，尾白

【同義詞】

clue, hint, indication, sign, signal

curly　　a.　蜷曲的；蜷縮的

【同義詞】

wavy, curled, kinky, frizzy

cyclist　　n.　騎腳踏車的人

【同義詞】

biker, bicyclist

D

dairy　　n.　乳品店；牛奶及乳品業

【同義詞】

creamery, dairy factory, dairy farm

damp　　a.　有濕氣的；潮濕的　　Track**46**

【同義詞】

moist, wettish, watery, dank

dare　　v.　敢；竟敢

【同義詞】

brave, meet, face, sustain

dash　　v.　猛撞；猛砸；擊碎

【同義詞】

hurry, rush, dart

daylight　　n.　日光；白晝

【同義詞】

light, sun, daylight hours

deadline　　n.　截止期限，最後限期

【同義詞】

time limit

decade　　n.　十；十年

【同義詞】

X, ten

decision　　n.　決定，決心；判斷；結論

【同義詞】

settlement, resolution, determination, ruling

declare n. 宣佈，宣告；聲明

【同義詞】

state, assert, announce, affirm

decoration n. 裝飾，裝潢

【同義詞】

adornment, ornamentation, embellishment, garnishment

defeat v. 戰勝，擊敗

【同義詞】

overcome, win, triumph, surpass

defend v. 防禦；保衛；保護

【同義詞】

protect, safeguard, shield, support

definitely adv. 明確地；明顯地，清楚地

【同義詞】

absolutely, assuredly, certainly, decidedly

delete v. 刪除；劃掉（文字等）；擦去

【同義詞】

cancel, remove

delicate a. 脆的，易碎的；嬌貴的

【同義詞】

mild, soft, fine, exquisite

delight v. 欣喜，愉快

【同義詞】

gratify, gladden, please, cheer

Track**47**

delivery n. 投遞，傳送

【同義詞】

transferal, transference, transmission, dispatch

demand v. 要求，請求

【同義詞】

ask, inquire, require

demonstration n. 證明，示範

【同義詞】

demo, display, evidence, illustration, proof, show

dense a. 密集的，稠密的

【同義詞】

crowded, packed, compact, thick

depart v. 起程，出發；離開，離去

【同義詞】

leave, exit, withdraw, go away

dependable a. 可靠的；可信任的

【同義詞】

trustworthy, honest, honorable

depression n. 沮喪，意氣消沈；不景氣，蕭條（期）

【同義詞】

despair, gloom, melancholy, pessimism, recession, sadness

description　　n.　描寫；敘述；形容

【同義詞】

portrayal, category, illustrative, depiction

deserve　　v.　應受，該得

【同義詞】

be worth, be worthy, earn, justify, merit, rate, warrant

designer　　n.　設計者；構思者；時裝設計師

【同義詞】

creator, inventor, deviser, artificer

desperate　　a.　情急拼命的，鋌而走險的

【同義詞】

frantic, wild, reckless, rash

destroy　　v.　毀壞，破壞

【同義詞】

abolish, demolish, eradicate, overthrow, overturn

detail　　n.　細節；詳情；瑣事；枝節

【同義詞】

element, feature, item, specification

detective　　n.　偵探；私家偵探

【同義詞】

investigator, private investigator, private eye

detergent　　n.　洗潔劑，洗衣粉

【同義詞】

Track**48**

cleaner, cleanser

determination　　n.　堅定；果斷，決斷力

【同義詞】

decision, solution

development　　n.　生長；進化；發展；發達

【同義詞】

growth, evolution, expansion, enlargement

device　　n.　設備，儀器，裝置

【同義詞】

machine, apparatus, tool, instrument

dialect　　n.　方言，土話

【同義詞】

speech, idiom, localism, provincialism

dialog　　n.　對話；交談

【同義詞】

conversation, talk, speech, words

dictation　　n.　口述；聽寫

【同義詞】

command, charge, order, injunction

中級 Listening Comprehension & Speaking
新制全民英檢
GEPT
The General English Proficiency Test [Intermediate]
NEW
聽力&口說 模擬試題+解答

Track**49**

| **digest** | v. | 消化（食物） |

【同義詞】

absorb, ingest, understand, comprehend

| **diploma** | n. | 畢業文憑，學位證書 |

【同義詞】

degree, academic title, certificate

| **dirt** | n. | 污物；爛泥；灰塵 |

【同義詞】

filth, grime, smudge

| **disagree** | v. | 不一致，不符 |

【同義詞】

differ, quarrel, conflict, dispute

| **disappointment** | n. | 失望；掃興，沮喪 |

【同義詞】

nonfulfillment, nonsuccess, failure, thwarting

| **disco** | n. | 小舞廳；迪斯科舞廳 |

【同義詞】

discotheque, disco music

| **discovery** | n. | 發現 |

【同義詞】

detection, unearthing, uncovering

| **disease** | n. | 病，疾病 |

【同義詞】

sickness, illness, ailment, malady

disgust　　n.　作嘔

Track**49**

【同義詞】

sicken, offend, repel, revolt

dislike　　v.　不喜愛，厭惡

【同義詞】

mislike, disrelish, disfavour, object to

distant　　n.　遠的；久遠的；遠離的

【同義詞】

remote, afar, abroad, out-of-the-way

district　　n.　區，轄區，行政區

【同義詞】

region, area, zone, territory

divorce　　v.　離婚

【同義詞】

separate, disjoin, divide, disconnect

donate　　v.　捐獻，捐贈

【同義詞】

give, contribute, present, bestow

dormitory　　n.　大寢室，團體寢室

【同義詞】

中級 Listening Comprehension & Speaking

NEW

新制全民英檢

GEPT

The General English Proficiency Test | Intermediate |

聽力&口說 模擬試題 +解答

Track**50**

dorm, student residence

doubtful　　a.　懷疑的；疑惑的

【同義詞】

uncertain, unsure, dubious, unbelieving

drag　　v.　拉，拖

【同義詞】

pull, draw, haul, tow

dramatic　　a.　戲劇的；劇本的

【同義詞】

theatrical, theatric

drawing　　n.　描繪，素描；製圖

【同義詞】

sketch, tracing, design, representation

drift　　v.　漂，漂流

【同義詞】

float, wander, roam, stray

drown　　v.　淹沒，浸濕

【同義詞】

submerge, sink, immerse, inundate

drunk　　a.　喝醉的

【同義詞】

intoxicated, tipsy, dizzy

due a. 應支付的；欠款的

【同義詞】

indebted, owed, payable, unpaid

Track**50**

dump v. 傾倒；拋棄

【同義詞】

empty, unload, discharge, discard

dynamic a. 力的；動力的

【同義詞】

active, energetic, forceful, strong

E

eager a. 熱心的，熱切的

【同義詞】

wanting, wishing, desirous, anxious

earn v. 賺得，掙得

【同義詞】

get, gain, obtain, make

earnest a. 認真的，誠摯的；重要的，嚴肅的

【同義詞】

determined, sincere, serious, devoted

earthquake n. 地震

中級 Listening Comprehension & Speaking
NEW
新制全民英檢
GEPT
The General English Proficiency Test [Intermediate]
聽力&口說 模擬試題 +解答

Track**51**

【同義詞】

seism, seismism, microseism, shock

ease　　v.　減輕，緩和

【同義詞】

relieve, reduce, soothe, allay

economy　　n.　節約，節省

【同義詞】

thrift, frugality, saving

edit　　v.　編輯；校訂

【同義詞】

correct, check, rewrite, revise

education　　n.　教育；培養；訓練

【同義詞】

teaching, instruction, tuition, nurture

efficient　　a.　效率高的；有能力的，能勝任的

【同義詞】

efficacious, effectual, effective, valid

elbow　　n.　肘部

【同義詞】

bend, right angle, jostle, hustle

elderly　　n.　年長的；上了年紀的

【同義詞】

old, rather old, oldish, venerable

elect   v.   選舉；推選

【同義詞】

choose, pick, select, appoint

Track**51**

elegant   a.   雅緻的，優美的，漂亮的

【同義詞】

graceful, polished, refined

elemental   a.   自然力的；基本的，原始的

【同義詞】

elementary, essential, fundamental, vital

elevator   n.   電梯；升降機

【同義詞】

escalator, moving stairs, lift

emergence   n.   出現；浮現；露頭

【同義詞】

issue, issuance, outpouring, efflux

emotional   a.   感情的

【同義詞】

emotive, affective, sensitive, sentient

employment   n.   雇用；受雇

【同義詞】

work, job, service, position

中級 Listening Comprehension & Speaking
NEW
新制全民英檢
GEPT
The General English Proficiency Test [Intermediate]
聽力&口說 模擬試題 +解答

Track**52**

encouragement n.　鼓勵；獎勵；促進

【同義詞】

cheer, promotion, support

engineer　　n.　工程師

【同義詞】

technician, technologist

entertainment　　n.　招待，款待

【同義詞】

amusement, diversion, distraction

evidence　　n.　證據；證詞；證人；物證

【同義詞】

facts, proof, grounds, data

exaggeration　　n.　誇張，誇大

【同義詞】

overstatement, magnification, puffery, amplification

examination　　n.　檢查，調查

【同義詞】

scrutiny, scrutinization, inspection

excellence　　n.　優秀；傑出；卓越

【同義詞】

brilliance, distinction, greatness

exchange　　v.　交換；調換；兌換

【同義詞】

change, interchange, substitute, switch

expression　　n.　表達；表示

Track**52**

【同義詞】

verbalization, pronouncement, communication, informing

extreme　　a.　末端的，盡頭的

【同義詞】

extravagant, excessive, exaggerated, overdone

F

facility　　n.　能力；技能

【同義詞】

edifice, building, structure, plant

fade　　v.　褪色，消退；凋謝

【同義詞】

dim, pale, dull, disappear

fail　　v.　不及格；失敗

【同義詞】

fall, flunk, be unsuccessful

faint　　v.　頭暈的，行將昏厥的

【同義詞】

中級 Listening Comprehension & Speaking
NEW
新制全民英檢
GEPT
The General English Proficiency Test [Intermediate]
聽力&口說 模擬試題+解答

Track**53**

swoon, weaken, black out

| **fake** | n. | 偽造；捏造；冒充者，騙子 |

【同義詞】

imitation, counterfeit

| **fame** | n. | 聲譽，名望 |

【同義詞】

reputation, name, renown, glory

| **familiar** | a. | 世所周知的；熟悉的；常見的；普通的 |

【同義詞】

popular, well-known, friendly, close

| **fare** | v. | 吃，進食；過活；遭遇；進展 |

【同義詞】

eat, be fed, prosper, progress

| **farewell** | n. | 再會！告別 |

【同義詞】

cheerio, good-by, good day, so long

| **fascinate** | v. | 迷住，使神魂顛倒；強烈地吸引 |

【同義詞】

interest, excite, attract, enthrall

| **feast** | n. | 盛宴，筵席 |

【同義詞】

enjoy, like, love, appreciate

feedback　　n.　回饋，反映

【同義詞】

answer, reaction, reply, response

Track**53**

fiction　　n.　小說

【同義詞】

fantasy, untruth, invention, legend

flexible　a.　可彎曲的，易彎曲的；柔韌的；有彈性的

【同義詞】

pliable, pliant, flexile, tractile

fluent　　a.　流利的，流暢的

【同義詞】

eloquent, articulate, glib, slick

folk　　n.　（某一民族或社會階層中的）廣大成員...

【同義詞】

people, persons, society, public

fortunate　a.　幸運的，僥倖的

【同義詞】

lucky, auspicious, providential

fortune　　n.　財產，財富；巨款

【同義詞】

riches, wealth, prosperity, treasure

fountain　　n.　泉水；噴泉；水源

中級 Listening Comprehension & Speaking
NEW
新制全民英檢
GEPT
The General English Proficiency Test [Intermediate]
聽力&口說 模擬試題 +解答

Track**54**

【同義詞】

spring, spout, spray, source

freeze　　v.　結冰，凝固

【同義詞】

chill, refrigerate, stiffen

frequent　　a.　時常發生的，頻繁的；屢次的

【同義詞】

common, constant, recurrent, regular, repeated

G

gang　　n.　（歹徒等的）一幫，一群

【同義詞】

group, crew, ring, band

glance　　n.　一瞥；掃視

【同義詞】

look, glimpse, skim

global　　a.　球狀的

【同義詞】

world-wide, universal, extensive, broad

gossip　　n.　閒話，聊天；流言蜚語

【同義詞】

chat, talk, prattle, tattle

grab v. 攫取，抓取

【同義詞】

Track**54**

snatch, seize, grasp, grip

grocery n. 食品雜貨店

【同義詞】

market

guarantee v. 保證，擔保

【同義詞】

promise, secure, pledge, swear

H

handicap n. 障礙，不利條件

【同義詞】

hindrance, burden, disadvantage, load

handy a. 手邊的；近便的

【同義詞】

useful, convenient, nearby, available

harm n. 損傷，傷害；危害

【同義詞】

damage, injury, loss

中級 Listening Comprehension & Speaking
NEW
新制全民英檢
GEPT
The General English Proficiency Test [Intermediate]
聽力&口說 模擬試題+解答

Track**55**

hint　　v.　暗示

【同義詞】

suggest, imply, allude

horror　　n.　恐怖，震驚

【同義詞】

fear, abhorrence, terror, dread

household　　n.　一家人；家眷；家庭，戶

【同義詞】

family, brood, folks

ideal　　a.　理想的，完美的

【同義詞】

perfect, faultless, flawless, model

illegal　　a.　不合法的，非法的；違反規則的

【同義詞】

unlawful, criminal, illegitimate

imagination　　n.　想像力；創造力

【同義詞】

dream, fancy, fantasy

imitate　　v.　模仿

【同義詞】

follow, trace, copy, duplicate

immediate　　a.　立即的，即刻的

Track**55**

【同義詞】

direct, instant, prompt, urgent

imply　　v.　暗指；暗示；意味著

【同義詞】

suggest, hint, infer

impress　　v.　給 ... 極深的印象；使感動

【同義詞】

affect, strike, fix, establish

incident　　n.　事件；事變

【同義詞】

happening, event, occurrence, adventure

independence　　n.　獨立；自主；自立

【同義詞】

autonomy, freedom, liberty, self-reliance, sovereignty

influence　　v.　影響，作用

【同義詞】

sway, affect, move, induce

informal　　a.　非正式的，非正規的

【同義詞】

中級 Listening Comprehension & Speaking
NEW
新制全民英檢
GEPT 聽力&口說 模擬試題 +解答
The General English Proficiency Test | Intermediate |

Track**56**

casual, cozy, easy, familiar, relaxed

ingredient n. （混合物的）組成部分；（烹調的）原料

【同義詞】

component, element, factor, item, part

injure v. 傷害；損害；毀壞

【同義詞】

damage, harm, hurt, wound

input n. 投入；輸入

【同義詞】

stimulant, stimulation, stimulus

insert v. 插入；嵌入

【同義詞】

introduce, inject, enter, put in

instead adv. 作為，替代

【同義詞】

in place of, rather than

instruction n. 教學，講授；教育

【同義詞】

advice, education, guidance, lecture, lesson

insult n. 侮辱，羞辱

【同義詞】

abuse, dishonor, offense

intermediate　　a.　中間的，居中的；中型的

【同義詞】

middle, intervening, in between

interpret　　v.　解釋，說明，詮釋

【同義詞】

explain, clarify, translate, analyze

interrupt　　v.　打斷，中斷

【同義詞】

discontinue, disrupt, disturb, intrude, pause

invention　　n.　發明，創造

【同義詞】

creation, design, device

J

jealous　　a.　妒忌的

Track**56**

【同義詞】

envious, covetous, desirous of

journey　　n.　旅行

【同義詞】

trip, voyage, tour, expedition

joyful　　a.　高興的，充滿喜悅的；使人高興的

【同義詞】

glad, happy, cheerful, blissful

junior　　　a.　年紀較輕的

【同義詞】

younger, lower, lesser, secondary

junk　　　n.　廢棄的舊物

【同義詞】

rubbish, trash, scrap, litter

justice　　　n.　正義；公平；正當的理由；合法

【同義詞】

fairness, fair play, impartiality, fair-mindedness

Track**57**

keen　　　a.　熱心的，熱衷的，深切的

【同義詞】

sharp, cutting, fine, acute

keyboard　　　n.　鍵盤

【同義詞】

keypad

kidnap　　　v.　誘拐

【同義詞】

snatch, abduct, carry off

kindness n. 仁慈；和藹；好意

【同義詞】

goodness, benevolence

kneel v. 跪下

【同義詞】

bow, kowtow

Track**57**

L

label n. 貼紙；標籤；商標

【同義詞】

name, brand, title, tag

labor n. 勞動

【同義詞】

work, employment, job, occupation

lack v. 不足，缺乏

【同義詞】

need, want

landlady n. 女房東；女主人

【同義詞】

proprietress, mistress

中級
Listening Comprehension & Speaking
NEW
新制全民英檢
GEPT 聽力&口說 模擬試題+解答
The General English Proficiency Test | Intermediate |

Track**58**

landlord n. 房東；主人

【同義詞】

owner, landowner, landholder, property-owner, proprietor

landmark n. 地標，陸標

【同義詞】

turning-point, milestone

landscape n. 風景，景色

【同義詞】

scene, aspect, outlook, prospect

laughter n. 笑；笑聲

【同義詞】

laugh, giggle, snicker

launch v. 使（船）下水；發射；發動，展開

【同義詞】

start, introduce, spring, set afloat

laundry n. 洗衣店；送洗的衣服

【同義詞】

wash, washing, dirty clothes

lawn n. 草坪，草地

【同義詞】

greensward, grassplot, grass, turf

leaflet n. 傳單；單張印刷品

【同義詞】

handbill, bill, brochure, pamphlet

leak v. 漏洞，裂縫

【同義詞】

drip, dribble, run out

leap v. 跳，跳躍

【同義詞】

jump, spring, vault, hop

lecture n. 授課；演講

【同義詞】

speech, talk, sermon, address

legend n. 傳說；傳奇故事；傳奇文學

【同義詞】

story, fiction, myth, fable

leisure n. 閒暇，空暇時間

【同義詞】

free time, spare time, rest, repose

liar n. 說謊的人

【同義詞】

fibber, falsifier, fabricator, perjurer

liberty n. 自由；自由權

【同義詞】

freedom, independence, autonomy, emancipation

librarian　n.　圖書館館長；圖書館員

【同義詞】

bibliothec, person in charge of a library

license　n.　許可，特許

【同義詞】

permission, allowance, consent

lifetime　n.　一生，終身

【同義詞】

life, lifespan

lighten　v.　變亮；發亮

【同義詞】

brighten, cheer, clear, illuminate, shine

limit　n.　界線；界限

【同義詞】

Track**59**

border, boundary, brink, limitation

lively　a.　精力充沛的；活潑的，輕快的

【同義詞】

exciting, bright, cheerful, vivid

load　n.　負載；負荷；憂慮

【同義詞】

burden, pressure, weight

loan   n.   借出；借出的東西
【同義詞】
advance, give

lobby   n.   大廳；門廊
【同義詞】
entrance, passageway, foyer

location   n.   位置；場所，所在地
【同義詞】
site, spot, point, locality

logical   a.   邏輯學的
【同義詞】
reasonable, sensible, sound, sane

loneliness   n.   孤獨，寂寞
【同義詞】
aloneness, desolation, isolation, lonesomeness

loose   a.   鬆的，寬的；鬆散的
【同義詞】
limp, drooping, unfastened, untied

lousy   a.   盡是蝨子的；不潔的
【同義詞】
dirty, filthy, miserable, rotten, stinky

loyal   a.   忠誠的，忠心的

中級 Listening Comprehension & Speaking
NEW
新制全民英檢
GEPT
The General English Proficiency Test [Intermediate]
聽力&口說 模擬試題 +解答

【同義詞】

trustworthy, devoted, faithful, constant

luxury   n.   奢侈，奢華

【同義詞】

luxuriousness, luxe, sumptuousness, lavishness

M

Track**60**

magical   a.   魔術的，魔法的

【同義詞】

charming, enchanting, witching

magnificent   a.   壯麗的，宏偉的，宏大的

【同義詞】

splendid, grand, stately, majestic

maintain   v.   保持，主張

【同義詞】

keep, uphold, possess, support

major   a.   較大的；主要的

【同義詞】

larger, greater, superior, higher

management   n.   管理；經營；處理

【同義詞】

administration, leadership, supervision

mature　　a.　成熟的，熟練的

【同義詞】

Track**60**

ripe, developed, mellow, fit, ready

mess　　v.　弄髒，弄亂；弄糟，毀壞

【同義詞】

dirty, disfigure, contaminate, pollute

method　　n.　方法，辦法

【同義詞】

system, way, manner, means, procedure

mild　　a.　溫和的，溫柔的

【同義詞】

gentle, kind, calm, warm

misunderstand　　v.　誤會；曲解

【同義詞】

misapprehend, misread, misconstrue, misconceive

modest　　a.　謙虛的，審慎的

【同義詞】

humble, bashful, shy, quiet

mood　　n.　心情，心境，情緒

【同義詞】

feeling, temperament, humor, disposition

Track**61**

native a. 天生的；本土的，本國的

【同義詞】

natural, original, indigenous

nearby a. 附近的

【同義詞】

around, close, near, neighboring

neat a. 整潔的；整齊的

【同義詞】

clean, orderly, trim, tidy

neglect v. 忽視，忽略

【同義詞】

overlook, disregard, ignore

neighborhood n. 鄰近地區

【同義詞】

district, region, surroundings

newcomer n. 新來的人；新近到達的移民

【同義詞】

beginner, greenhorn, novice, starter

nightmare n. 夢魘；惡夢

【同義詞】

ordeal, trial

O

Track**61**

obvious　　a.　明顯的；顯著的

【同義詞】

understandable, apparent, clear, plain

occasion　　n.　場合，時刻；重大活動，盛典

【同義詞】

time, instance, case, spot

option　　n.　選擇；選擇權；選擇自由

【同義詞】

choice, alternative, substitute, equivalent

oral　　a.　口頭的，口述的

【同義詞】

spoken, voiced, vocalized, sounded

origin　　n.　起源；由來；起因

【同義詞】

beginning, start, infancy, birth

outcome　　n.　結果；結局；後果

【同義詞】

result, consequence, effect, upshot

output　　n.　出產；生產

【同義詞】

turnout, production

中級 Listening Comprehension & Speaking
新制全民英檢
GEPT
The General English Proficiency Test [Intermediate]
NEW
聽力&口說 模擬試題 +解答

Track**62**

outstanding a. 顯著的；傑出的；重要的

【同義詞】

important, great, famous

overcome v. 戰勝；克服

【同義詞】

conquer, defeat, upset, overpower

overlook v. 看漏；忽略

【同義詞】

neglect, ignore, disregard, skip

overthrow v. 推翻，打倒；廢除

【同義詞】

upset, demolish, crush, beat, overpower

P

pace n. 速度；進度

【同義詞】

rate, speed, stride, walk

parade n. 行進，行列，遊行

【同義詞】

show, display, review

paradise n. 樂園，極樂

【同義詞】

heaven, bliss, glory, ecstasy

participate   v.   參加，參與

【同義詞】

partake, take part in, have a hand in, enter into

particularly   adv.   特別，尤其

【同義詞】

chiefly, especially, specially

partnership   n.   合夥或合作關係

【同義詞】

alliance, association, union

passion   n.   熱情，激情

【同義詞】

emotion, enthusiasm, craze, fervor

pat   v.   輕拍，輕打

【同義詞】

tap, stroke, rap

Track**63**

penalty   n.   處罰；刑罰

【同義詞】

punishment, penalty, sentence, condemnation

permission   n.   允許，許可，同意

【同義詞】

leave, consent, license

personality   n.   人格，品格

【同義詞】

identity, individuality

pity   n.   憐憫；同情

【同義詞】

sympathy, sorrow, compassion, mercy

possibly   adv.   也許，可能

【同義詞】

perhaps, maybe

postpone   v.   使延期，延遲，延緩

【同義詞】

delay, defer, suspend

present   a.   出席的，在場的

【同義詞】

actual, contemporary, current

previous   a.   先的，前的，以前的

【同義詞】

prior, earlier, former, preceding

probably   adv.   大概，或許，很可能

【同義詞】

likely, presumably, supposedly

promotion　　n.　提升，晉級

【同義詞】

advancement, improvement, lift, rise

property　　n.　財產，資產；所有物

【同義詞】

possession, holdings, belongings

Q

qualification　　n.　資格；能力

【同義詞】

competence, competency, fitness, satisfactoriness

quantity　　n.　量

【同義詞】

amount, number, sum, measure

quarrel　　v.　爭吵；不和；吵鬧

【同義詞】

argument, disagreement, fuss

quote　　v.　引用；引述

【同義詞】

cite, illustrate, repeat

Track**64**

Track**64**

recognition n. 認出，識別；認識

【同義詞】

identification, recollection, remembrance, recall

recovery n. 重獲；復得

【同義詞】

recapturing, retaking, retrieval

recreation n. 消遣；娛樂，遊戲

【同義詞】

play, amusement, entertainment, pleasure

reduce v. 減少；縮小；降低

【同義詞】

lessen, lower, decrease, diminish

reflect v. 反射；照出，映出

【同義詞】

mirror, send back

refresh v. 使清新，使清涼

【同義詞】

renew, revive, reanimate, regenerate

refuse v. 拒絕；拒受；不准

【同義詞】

decline, reject

relax v. 使鬆弛，使鬆懈，放鬆

【同義詞】

Track**65**

rest, loosen, ease up

rely v. 依靠，依賴；依仗

【同義詞】

trust, confide, depend on, count on

replace v. 把 . . . 放回；取代

【同義詞】

succeed, supply, come after, substitute for

represent v. 描繪；表示

【同義詞】

portray, depict, illustrate, symbolize

request v. 要求，請求

【同義詞】

apply, require

requirement n. 需要；必需品

【同義詞】

need, necessity, urgent need, must

rescue v. 援救；營救；挽救

【同義詞】

release, retrieve, salvage, redeem

中級 Listening Comprehension & Speaking
NEW
新制全民英檢
GEPT
The General English Proficiency Test | Intermediate |
聽力&口說 模擬試題+解答

Track**65**

responsibility n. 責任

【同義詞】

duty, obligation, office

S

scare v. 驚嚇，使恐懼

【同義詞】

frighten, alarm, startle, unnerve

schedule n. 表；清單；目錄

【同義詞】

list, index, post, slate

selection n. 選擇；選拔

【同義詞】

choosing, picking, hand-picking, singling out

significance n. 重要性，重要

【同義詞】

meaning, connotation, implication

sociable a. 好交際的；善交際的

【同義詞】

friendly, congenial, amiable, cordial

sorrow n. 悲痛，悲哀，悲傷，憂傷

【同義詞】

grief, sadness, regret, trouble

spiritual　　a.　精神的，心靈的

【同義詞】

religious, sacred, holy

splendid　　a.　有光彩的；燦爛的

【同義詞】

gorgeous, glorious, wonderful, magnificent

Track**66**

staff　　n.　全體職員，全體工作人員

【同義詞】

group, committee, personnel, crew

steady　　a.　穩固的，平穩的

【同義詞】

constant, fixed, inert, regular

strategy　　n.　戰略；戰略學

【同義詞】

planning, management, tactics, manipulation

strength　　n.　力量，力氣；實力；效力

【同義詞】

power, energy, force, vigor

suitable　　a.　適當的；合適的；適宜的

【同義詞】

中級 Listening Comprehension & Speaking
NEW
新制全民英檢
GEPT 聽力&口說 模擬試題+解答
The General English Proficiency Test | Intermediate |

Track**66**

fitting, proper, timely, favorable

suppose　　v.　猜想，以為

【同義詞】

believe, think, imagine, consider

surely　　adv.　確實，無疑，一定

【同義詞】

firmly, confidently, unhesitatingly

T

tasty　　a.　美味的；高雅的，大方的

【同義詞】

good-tasting, savory

temporary　　a.　臨時的；暫時的，一時的

【同義詞】

passing, momentary, transient, short-lived

tend　　v.　照管，照料；護理；管理

【同義詞】

attend, administer, help, mind

tendency　　n.　傾向；癖性；天分

【同義詞】

inclination, leaning, bent

tender   a.   嫩的 ; 柔軟的

【同義詞】

soft, delicate, gentle, kind

thankful   a.   感謝的 , 感激的 ; 欣慰的

【同義詞】

indebted, grateful, appreciative, obliged

thorough   a.   徹底的 ; 完全的

【同義詞】

complete, intensive, full, sweeping

Track**67**

thoughtful   a.   深思的 , 沈思的

【同義詞】

kind, considerate, sympathetic, concerned

timid   a.   膽小的 , 易受驚的

【同義詞】

shy, bashful, meek

transfer   v.   搬 ; 轉換 ; 調動

【同義詞】

deliver, pass, hand over, sign over

transform   v.   使改變 ; 使改觀 ; 將 ... 改成

【同義詞】

change, convert, alter

typical   a.   典型的 , 有代表性的

【同義詞】

representative, symbolic, characteristic, distinctive

Track**67**

understanding   n.   了解；理解；領會；認識

【同義詞】

comprehension, cognition, consciousness

undertake   v.   試圖；著手做；進行，從事

【同義詞】

try, attempt, endeavor

upset   v.   弄翻，打翻；傾覆

【同義詞】

overturn, unsettle, capsize, tip over

urge   v.   催促；力勸；激勵；慫恿

【同義詞】

push, force, drive, plead

urgent   a.   緊急的，急迫的

【同義詞】

pressing, important, imperative, compelling

usage   n.   使用，用法；處理

【同義詞】

method, practice, way, use

Track**68**

V

vacant　　a.　空的；空白的

【同義詞】

unoccupied, empty, void, blank

vague　　a.　模糊不清的，朦朧的

【同義詞】

unclear, indistinct, indefinite

vain　　a.　愛虛榮的，自負的，炫耀的

【同義詞】

unsuccessful, ineffectual, futile, fruitless

valid　　a.　合法的；有效的；妥當的

【同義詞】

legal, effective, just

valuable　　a.　值錢的，貴重的

【同義詞】

costly, expensive, high-priced

vanish　　v.　突然不見；消失

【同義詞】

disappear, fade, perish, go away

313

Track**68**

vary　　　v.　使不同；變更；修改

【同義詞】

change, differ, alter, deviate

vast　　　a.　廣闊的，浩瀚的，廣大的

【同義詞】

large, immense, great, enormous

verbal　　a.　言辭上的；言語的，字句的

【同義詞】

oral, spoken, said

violate　　v.　違犯；違背，違反

【同義詞】

break, trespass, infringe

vital　　　a.　生命的；維持生命所必需的

【同義詞】

necessary, important, essential, fundamental

vivid　　　a.　鮮豔的；鮮明的

【同義詞】

bright, brilliant, strong, clear

voluntary　　a.　自願的，志願的

【同義詞】

intentional, intended

voyage　　n.　航海，航行，乘船旅遊

【同義詞】

journey, migration, passage, tour, travel, trip

wage　　n.　薪水；報酬

【同義詞】

pay, payment, salary

warmth　　n.　溫暖

【同義詞】

fervidity, vehemence, zeal

warn　　v.　警告；告誡；提醒

【同義詞】

inform, notify, caution

wealthy　　a.　富的；富裕的；豐富的

【同義詞】

rich, affluent, prosperous, moneyed

withdraw　　v.　抽回；拉開；移開

【同義詞】

retreat, recede, retire, quit

worthwhile　　a.　值得做的

【同義詞】

meaningful, useful, valuable, worthy

wrestle　　v.　摔角

【同義詞】

struggle, battle, fight

 Y

yard　　n.　院子；天井；庭院

【同義詞】

court, courtyard, inner court, quadrangle

year　　n.　年，一年

【同義詞】

session, period, space, term

yearn　　v.　渴望；嚮往

【同義詞】

desire, crave, long for, wish for

yell　　v.　叫喊；吼叫聲

【同義詞】

call, cry, bawl, exclaim

yield　　v.　生產；產生

【同義詞】

produce, give, grant, bear

yoke　　n.　軛，牛軛

【同義詞】

harness, shackle, bridle

youngster　　n.　小孩

【同義詞】

child, minor, youth, kid

Z

zealous　　a.　熱心的；狂熱的

【同義詞】

enthusiastic, fervent, earnest, ardent

Track**70**

zero　　n.　零；零號

【同義詞】

nothing, naught, nil, none

zip　　n.　子彈等飛射聲，撕布聲；活力，精力

【同義詞】

vigor, energy, vitality

zone　　n.　地帶；地區

【同義詞】

region, area, territory, place

國家圖書館出版品預行編目資料

NEW GEPT新制全民英檢(中級)：聽力&口說模擬試題+解答
／張文娟著. -- 初版. -- 新北市：
雅典文化事業有限公司，民111.10 面； 公分
ISBN 978-626-96423-0-4(平裝)
1.CST: 英語 2.CST: 能力測驗
805.1892 111011833

英語工具書系列 18

NEW GEPT新制全民英檢(中級)： 聽力&口說模擬試題+解答

作者／張文娟
責編／張文娟
美術編輯／姚恩涵
封面設計／林鈺恆

法律顧問：方圓法律事務所／涂成樞律師

總經銷：永續圖書有限公司
永續圖書線上購物網
www.foreverbooks.com.tw

雲端回函卡

出版日／2022年10月

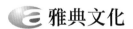

雅典文化

出版社	22103 新北市汐止區大同路三段194號9樓之1
	TEL （02）8647-3663
	FAX （02）8647-3660